CREATIVE SURGERY

CLELIA FARRIS

TRANSLATED BY
RACHEL S. CORDASCO
AND
JENNIFER DELARE

ROSARIUM

CREATIVE SURGERY

CONTENTS

A Day to Remember

"Pink lobsters!"

"Murena, all crustaceans are pink now."

"And I want them red. Like when I was a kid."

Olì took up the electronic brush, chose a color from the menu palette, and mixed coral red, lemon yellow, and a bit of white to obtain the color called "Ceruti" by Giacomo Ceruti, author of *Still Life with Shrimp*. Shrimp, lobsters, same family.

With small overlapping touches, she changed the lobster's color in the image projected on the white wall. More than once, Ceruti's work had saved her: the beige taken from the nuts, the right shade of Spadone pears, the roughness of the boiled kale—his works, five centuries old, but still vivid and bright.

Brushing it with her fingertips, she turned the mnemonic sphere, and the subjective image changed. From the fish tray, which was served at his nephew's baptism, Murena's gaze shifted to a young athlete with curly hair, intent on chewing a roasted pig's ear.

"Well, look who it is," Murena said. "That cheat, Curcaio. I want him erased. Shoo. Disappear."

"You want to erase your son?"

"Bastard."

"But he's the father of your nephew, the child you have baptized."

"So what? Three months ago, that wretch cheated me with that motor boat deal. Already we are ... could you also remove the memory of just how much money I lost?"

"If I take it away, you'll stop hating him."

"Ah."

"Let's do it like this: brighten the sun's light, remove the oil stain from your pants, erase your brother-in-law's comment, *When will you give me the lobster pot?*, and replace it with *Keep your lobster pot clean; at the moment I don't need it.* But the memory of Curcaio's presence remains. I can fade it a little with a filter, so it won't be so strong. You'll have to make an effort, to remind yourself who he is."

"Perfect. You like eels?"

Olì closed her eyes: Giacomo Ceruti's nickname was "the Little Beggar."

"They're big?"

"As big as my arm!"

"Anchovies?" asked Impiastera, stretching her neck toward the frying pan.

"Murena came to fix a recent memory."

"Ah, Murena. That son of cheaters and parent of cheaters."

"The thin eels are tastier," retorted Olì, with a thrill of pride.

"And what is this?"

Shifting aside an embroidered curtain, Impiastera revealed a sex doll assembled out of padded jackets and pants. Several loops of a scarf supported a yellow woolen balaclava, fitted onto a large, empty coconut, hidden in part by dark sunglasses.

"Garbage," Olì replied, slamming the dishes on the table.

She was ashamed because, occasionally at night, she embraced the doll in search of a soft body.

"You could call her 'Nostalgia.'"

"Nostalgia for what?"

"For 'algos'—pain, and 'nostos'—return. The pain of return. Every memory is a little painful for us because we know that we cannot go back to that time."

"How boring! If you don't stop, I'll erase your memories of ancient Greek."

"Seriously? But that's my grandma's heritage."

"That's helpful. There's a great demand for interpreters."

"You should get back to sculpting, or painting on that electronic canvas."

"Sit down, it's ready."

Impiastera took a seat at the table. Silently, she devoured the pieces of fried eel, the seaweed salad, and a container of purslane. She wiped her mouth with a fine linen napkin and hastened to unwrap the dessert with her hands. Impiastera's rock was right next door. They met each other often to chat and exchange courtesies. Olì had even asked her to become her wife in death. Who would bury her when the time came? There were people who didn't worry about wasting away on this rock, in the position in which death caught them. Not her. She wanted a burial as it should be, with fire. Impiastera would put her on the boat, sprinkle her with alcohol, and set her on fire. She would drift, a flaming shell on the blue waters of Santa Igia. A beautiful end. An artistic end.

"In the holy name of Dagon!"

Her friend had brought to the table an emerald green cake covered in transparent jelly.

"My latest creation. Chlorophyll algae flour, white turnips, dates, and avocado cream."

Every ten days Impiastera produced a new dessert. Olì was her guinea pig.

"Flavor?" Her friend wrote down every impression on a spreadsheet.

Olì passed the bite of cake from one cheek to the other.

"Slimy moss. There are some ..."

"... candied clams in the middle."

Olì clapped her hand on her mouth, rose, and ran to spit the salty bolus into the trashcan.

To be reviewed, Impiastera wrote. "Maybe I can remove the clams and add a decoration of real pearls ..."

"Is someone coming?"

Olì walked to a window. Above a large speedboat with its engine on, the bow raised above the water, and the prow loaded with oysters, was Curcaio, who gave her a sparkling smile.

"Olì, fairy of Memory, can you make my memories brighter?"

"You want to take away the memory of Murena from your son's baptism."

"That old bully ruined my party! The best fish of San Michele and he was going around telling the guests that it was all rotten!"

Olì smiled.

"I want five lobsters."

Two days later, the radio trilled.

Olì had gone downstairs to check the nets. Many years before, the sea had smashed the door of the building, flooded the cellars, filled the elevator, and risen to the fifth floor. The other tenants had already fled, so she and her mother had moved to the top floor. Now the water lapped the steps of the stairs that led to the sixth-floor landing, nourishing a carpet of viscous algae, barnacles, and anemones with long tentacles.

In the nets she often found some mackerel, trills, and small bream, which supplemented her diet of edible algae and plums. They picked the plums from the trees that grew on the building's roof, now covered with earth.

She wiped her hands on her sarong with some apprehension. She was always afraid to receive a call from Castello. She pressed the answer button.

"Yes, this is Olì of San Michele."

"I'm Massimeh. God told me to call you."

"What do you need?"

"Nothing for me. God needs you. Bring your magic ball."

Removing the fish from the nets, she threw back into the water those with a suspicious blue stain on the muzzle and kept the others in a bucket full of fresh water. She was still inspecting the nets when a small octopus came out of a submerged jar and wrapped her wrist in its tentacles. She considered the ease with which she could have captured it and hung it in the bucket, then laughed at the tickle of those elastic fingers. How soft they were! The suckers pressed delicately on her skin and then retracted in a ballet of affectionate little touches—almost like an animal, in the shape of Olì's hand, had recognized a companion and wanted to speak to it.

With a dense mesh screen, Olì pulled a handful of silver fish out of the bucket and handed one of them to the octopus, which grabbed it by wrapping it with a tentacle and making it disappear beneath his head, where his mouth was.

"Good Sar."

On the jar in which the octopus had burrowed was text that read: *C sar.* C for *casa*—Sar's house.

She freed herself from the animal's grip, put it back in the water, and went back upstairs. She wore a hat of woven algae, bound it under her chin, and unmoored the boat—an old fridge filled with floating foam—on which she had tied a car seat. Two mudguards on the sides made it more stable and functioned like counterweights. She started out slowly, stroking the oars toward the hospital. The heat of the sun made the water heavy, viscous. Below the surface she could see the squared platforms of submerged houses, on which pink and yellow madrepore grew extensively along with tufts of algae and white coral. She made a wide turn, so as not to stick the oars in the antennae, often invisible under the layers of moss that covered them. She passed Deledda Rock, the last immersed area before the Big Pit. A few strokes, and she was in the shadow of the hospital.

The upper three floors of the building emerged from the water. She approached a smashed window, tied the boat to an iron spike, and lifted herself on to the windowsill. The interior was a succession of empty rooms—beds, machinery, even the door frames, everything had been plundered. Climbing up from an inner stairway, Massimeh lived within the helicopter, on top of the roof. As long as the gas lasted, he had been shuttling between the Castle and the various quarters of the city, carrying letters, exchanging fishing hooks and lines derived from medical instruments in plastic receptacles. When the carburator died, Massimeh had started to build small short-range radios. He dove into the lower floors and found rust-free stainless steel sheets, copper cables, plastics, and cutting tools. He carved transceiver shells out of the driftwood. They even came from Accoddi to buy them in exchange for obsidian tools and coconut oil.

Olì came to the roof and Massimeh, tall, dark, and solemn, met her with open arms.

"God loves you!"

"Enough to pay me for the work?"

"God has great esteem for your work, Olì. You bring joy to the memories of each of us. Just yesterday, on this terrace, there was a beautiful gathering. We sang His praises and invoked happiness for everyone."

Olì opened the briefcase and spread the equipment out on a hospital stretcher.

"Lie down."

Massimeh lay down on his back, on an operating room table, and lifted his black t-shirt, faded from the sun. Olì stuck the glass ball in his navel and activated a connection with the computer.

"Think hard about yesterday's gathering."

Massimeh closed his eyes, and after a few seconds the sphere projected the images onto the curved helicopter wall. Olì turned it gently with her finger until the images were clear. The "great gathering" constituted five people kneeling in prayer before Massimeh, who officiated at the mass, using fish meal and palm wine.

"What do you want me to do?"

"Tzugata, Priogu, and Nubedicorallo would like to participate, but they are stuck on their rocks, so God wouldn't be offended if we added some more people to the memory."

Olì really doubted that a freak like Tzugata had the capacity to concentrate for the duration of a religious service.

"Could you also draw in some strangers?"

"Yes, of course."

Olì opened the file "human figures" in the database and selected "kneeling." She cut some characters from Caravaggio, some seventeenth-century adorations, and some miracles of the saints. All in all, the clothing was similar to that of Massimeh's followers—shaved heads, threadbare pants, dirty hands—and she pasted them into the empty spaces of the memory between one of the faithful and another.

The projected memory was filled with new kneeling followers, some with their hands folded, others with bowed heads, and still others with an ecstatic look directed at Massimeh.

"Beautiful! Beautiful! More, put in more, fill up the terrace!"

"It'll cost you."

"Doesn't matter! It's enough just to see so many heads!"

Heads! That's the solution! There was no need to characterize each fake individual. From a certain distance the human eye ignores the differences, perceives two eyes only in a vague way, a nose, a forehead. She cut the faces of the first row below the nose and pasted them behind the group of followers; she then cut a strip from the faces and placed it behind them. In a few moves the roof of the hospital was populated by a crowd of men and women in prayer.

While Olì put away her instruments, Massimeh dug around under the helicopter seats, scattering spreadsheets everywhere like white butterfly wings.

"I can give you one of my sermons. I wrote it just yesterday ..."

"I'd prefer a few pounds of clams," Olì replied. Among Massimeh's followers was Monia, a mussel farmer.

"Here it is! It's called *Brothers and Sisters Living Together with Joy*. Or you can have a watch."

"The watch, thanks."

We live together in joy. Only Massimeh could believe that they were still a community.

As she rode back to her rock, Olì let her gaze drift. A mussel farmer with a basket under her arm collected mussels on top of a building, skipping across the gaps between one parapet and the other. The currents had accumulated earth and waste around the tops of the tallest buildings, forming conical islands, similar to many small volcanoes emerging from the water. Every accumulation of earth possessed an inhabitant, the lonely castaway of the old jokes, a comparison made even more apt by the coconut trees that grew on the islands. Each tenant's bed, a hammock, swayed among the trunks.

Even the terraces of the hill of San Michele shone with water dotted with green rice seedlings. The hill was one of the few places where, instead of a single individual, you found an entire family of seven living. They possessed a small desalinator, so they managed to grow rice. All the others got drinking water through sycamore trees, which collected humidity from the air.

She then remembered that her sycamore wasn't working well. The last time she'd looked at the tank level, she'd found it half full. She stopped at home just to take a full water bottle and a wider hat. The afternoon sun flared blindingly from the water. She moved toward Oja's rock.

Oja Mommìa was the best sycamore technician in the area, but he refused to own a radio. "Hope for a warning, eh? And this is what you want. You want me to call you before the catastrophe takes place. That's fresh! We will all die—and in silence!"

To hire him to repair the tree meant to sit through a speech on "the slow assassin," as he called it: the sea. Mommìa spent much of his time measuring the water level. He was old enough to remember the Night of the First Wave, when the sea suddenly rose up and submerged the Marina and Santa Avendrace. Dozens of people quietly sleeping in their beds had drowned.

She had postponed her visit to Oja because, to reach his rock, she had to pass right by Argentiera, a dangerous place.

The sea forced her to follow well-defined routes. That jumble of recovered material—call it a "boat"—was cobbled together and could tip over or sink at any moment. Best if it was in low water half a mile from the terrace of a building on which one could stand.

She had just passed the Falletti rocks when the right mudguard fender crashed against something submerged. Olì rowed backwards and out of the water appeared a shark fin.

"Hands up!" said a voice at her shoulder.

Behind her, three old people astride plastic tanks leveled yellow and green toy rifles at her. The black chasms of their pupils frightened her. The shark emerged, an accomplice in a scuba suit, with a fin pasted onto the cap. The man grabbed at the corner of the fridge and made it lean toward the water, threatening to overturn it. Behind the lens of the mask, Olì caught an amused glitter of evil.

The rifles contained water—or at worst, piss—but the old ones, who had shed their inhibitions with age, were further excited by drugs, whose use was only permitted to those who had reached seventy. Their reactions were unpredictable. They might rob you and laugh or drown you with equal hilarity.

"Give us everything you have," an old man said.

Olì drew out the watch bag that Massimeh had given her and placed it on the oar, stretching it toward the robbers.

"It's a precious object to me," she lied.

The really precious object was the memory computer, which she always carried on herself, strapped around the bust, under her sarong.

At the sight of the watch, the old people glanced up and leaned forward to grab it, the shark-man arriving first, and Olì took the opportunity to paddle quickly away. She heard them arguing, screaming like gulls.

"Hey, you on the rock! Oja Mommìa, you there?"

A head shrunken by the sun, hairless, leaned through a gap between two axes of the house. So as not to lose sight of the plumb line, Oja let the house fall apart.

"Three millimeters! he answered.

"That's high tide."

"Three millimeters isn't high tide! It's a signal!"

At the top of the rusty ladder leading to the pier, Olì was welcomed by a slim, tanned girl. For a moment she thought it was Oja's younger daughter here for a visit; then she saw the tattoo with the Quattro Mori—the flag of Sardinia—on her shoulder, and she knew that it was Castello's councilwoman.

"I'm Elis," the girl said, introducing herself.

Too late to go back.

"Nice to meet you, Olì. I was just going to you, but I stopped by Mommìa's to finish some repairs to Castello's sycamores."

Olì stayed silent; the other had enough words for them both.

"We founded a new city council. We are young and full of ideas. To begin we want to restore the waste barge. It will be compulsory to own a bucket in which to perform bodily functions, and every three days the bucket barge will remove it."

The residents of San Michele would wipe their asses with that rule.

"We believe in Beauty, and we want to return Beauty to the people. You are still our 'community artist.' I was just a little girl, but I remember well your splendid intangible art. All over the world, artists of the likes of Paivi or Timaro carry on transversal art ..."

Olì contemplated the algae hat on the girl's head. Did she intend to give her a lesson?

"... the suggestions of fragrances blended with the purity of the sea's colors ..."

Mommìa was shaken from slumber.

"The sea! Three millimeters! Three millimeters more than yesterday at the same time!" he bellowed. And grabbing Elis by the arm, he dragged her to look with her own eyes at the stake in the seabed, on which he had carved various heights.

Olì walked away from them and onto the noisy pier constructed from a car door, up to the farthest corner, in which still hung the big organic battery spotlight that she had mounted many years ago. It took three months of calculations, verifications, and inspections to establish the exact coordinates of places on which the spotlights were to be installed. In the places where the sea was deep, she had to anchor a small raft to the seabed, and above it she tied the lamp and the devices that operated it. Four more months to mount the equipment, paddling every day from one point to another to adjust the triangulation, waiting for night to do the tests, one beam of light at a time, so as not to reveal the whole operation.

She had called it *Dream Time*.

Olì leaned her hand on the spotlight corroded by the salt and looked up at the heavens, as if her sculpture was still there, in the blue tissue of the sky.

It was inaugurated on Christmas night, twenty-eight degrees Celsius, a weak breeze out of the south, the stars clear and bright. The music and scents had calmed her. Rich twelve-tone shades full of tonalities and unpredictable, and a precious blend of bergamot, cistus labdanum, iris, rose, and jasmine in spray dispensers. The essences were synthetic, but the effect had been magnificent.

From her console she controlled each spotlight from a distance. The beams of colored light lit up according to a musical tempo, at first only three eighth notes on the treble clef and three pink ribbons in the sky, then slowly the sonorous and bright shapes had made entire landscapes appear—woods, mountains, prehistoric towers, hills. A flood of places that were now submerged, accompanied by their own earthy odors. So the lights had taken on the features of forgotten animals—horses, cows, and sheep—hundreds of small white explosions that remained fixed in the sky—accompanied by a shepherd. She had finished with bright Castello designs, their white and square towers, the flag with the Quattro Mori floating above the apparition.

The shrill squawking of a crow brought her back to the present, a present without art.

"We'd really like it if you wanted to resume creating for the community."

The young Elis reappeared at her side, silly and tenacious.

"Which community? Everyone only respects the rules of their rock. Do you of Castello really believe that an archipelago obeys you because you call yourselves the Communal Council?"

"Someone said, 'No man is an island'."

"I'm not really inspired," Olì said, cutting her short.

"Oh, that's not an obstacle. For us everything you create is good, as long as it's beautiful and leaves us all breathless."

I could invent a candy that sticks in your throat, Olì thought.

"If you need tools or specific materials, you can submit a request addressed to me ..."

"And do it before the sea rises again!" Oja added.

"I have three nice baskets of bananas, my dear. And I'll also add two cans of anti-rust. Your pier needs it."

Once again, Olì stared distrustfully at the old woman who had arrived at her rock together with a granddaughter right in the middle of the afternoon. A nuisance at the hottest hour, painted blue and white, with pupils that were too bright.

"What do you want from me?"

The old woman put an arm around her shoulders, and they moved away from the girl.

"The little one is always sad."

Olì resolutely removed the old arm and glanced at the girl. A fishbone had more flesh on it.

"She cries when she should laugh," she went on. "It's the fault of that stupid memory. You'll cleanse it, and we'll all be happier."

Blue-face said she was her grandmother, but Olì knew that sometimes newborns were sold in exchange for a lobster pot.

"The girl agrees?"

"You do your job, dear, and you'll be well rewarded."

"I need peace. Leave us alone."

"Perfect! Perfect!"

The old lady hobbled toward the ladder and disappeared. Shortly afterwards, Olì felt the buzz of an elastic-wrapped motor and the walnut shell with which the old woman skimmed forward, heading toward Tzugata's rock.

"What's your name?"

"Tilde," answered the girl. "I gave it to myself; I read it on a box."

"You want me to erase the memory that makes you sad?"

Tilde shrugged.

In fact, the old one was right. The girl had the air of one who believed that the world brings only disappointment.

"Well, let's take a look and then decide."

Too docile, Tilde lay on the couch, lowered her swimsuit, and let Olì insert the glass sphere into her navel.

"Think of the memory that saddens you, think with all your strength."

Tilde closed her eyes and clenched her fists. The sphere projected confused images. A sky filled with seagulls overlapped with two infant hands that ripped off the barnacles on the buildings with the help of a sharp oyster shell.

"Why are the seagulls making you sad?"

The girl kept her eyes closed.

"I wish I could fly. Like them. Fly away, leave."

Her eyelids trembled.

"The Earth is all water by now."

"North."

The fabulous north. It was said that beyond the thirtieth parallel there were cultivated fields and even houses built on dry land.

"And the barnacles?"

"When I'm hungry, my grandmother tells me to go find barnacles. I'm barefoot, and the shells hurt me."

The submerged halves of the buildings were populated with shoals of sharp barnacles. The girl had misunderstood the request and was showing her physical desires and sorrows.

"Tilde, what is the memory that, according to your grandmother, makes you sad?"

The barnacles vanished, the seagulls disappeared, the sky darkened into the color of lead. A faraway rumble and then an explosion of thunder. The smooth surface of the sea was pierced by pins, then the drops became more consistent and the rain poured down.

The little girl danced on a plastic jetty, and when she turned her eyes to the sky, a bunch of silver arrows converged on her. Murmuring a song, she splashed into the puddles with her bare feet and laughed. She rubbed her face and continued to laugh.

Olì keenly observed the sky's water, exaggerated, vivifying, she could almost feel the freshness on her skin.

The day of the thunderstorm had begun as any other day, hot as usual, calm as usual. Panting under the sun, Olì had reached Tzugata's rock.

Tzugata was always at home, spending most of his time swinging on a hammock. Whatever he wanted, it arrived by sea. His rock was a magnet for other boats because he alone had kept up the main activity of the district—the preparation of drugs derived from lichen hybrids.

Officially, his customers were the elderly in search of fun, but after sunset the age of the boats' occupants decreased like the tide. From the teak balustrade, Tzugata would stick out a rod, on which a basket was tied. From the boat the buyer put in the agreed-upon object—fresh food, fresh water, abbardente, sunscreen; sometimes, cat statues were enough; every kind of cat, curled up, seated, with an erect tail, with a movable head. Tzugata had fond memories of Perla, his rock companion, a Siamese with turquoise eyes that seemed to understand words and actions better than a human being.

After the exchange the customers would go home, to dream in a hammock of a world less liquid and less hot.

"I can intensify Perla's memory," Olì had told him from the boat.

Tzugata raised himself from his hammock.

"You can really do that?"

Olì had shown him a computer demonstration and the magic glass sphere.

"Every time you think about her, it will seem like she was just there, that you can caress her. You'll feel the softness of her fur and hear the exact intonation of her meow. Her eyes will look at you with that old adoration, and your fingers will send back the vibration of her purring."

"What do you want in return?"

Olì remained silent for a moment, staring at the smooth surface of the sea.

"I need something to aid in inspiration. Give me an idea, a brilliant one."

"Deal."

After receiving the treatment Tzugata had given her a can of tuna.

Olì had held it in her hands, perplexed. It was very light. *Too light* because there really was tuna in there.

"Puffer fish liver?"

Tzugata smiled.

"Eat it in small doses."

Returning to her own rock, Olì had opened the can. It contained fish eggs, mini gelatinous spheres that reminded her of, in a reduced version, the ball that she used to view memories. She looked for a teaspoon in the kitchen drawers and found a leather box that contained twelve pieces of silverware, lying in velvet. Forgotten by the previous owners.

Her hand trembled when she brought Tzugata's caviar to her mouth, such that some eggs remained on her lips and she had to push them in with her fingers. In contact with her palate, the eggs dissolved, spreading the taste of salt and sea. She sat at her project table in front of the designs of vortices of musical water and coral reefs made out of fiberglass.

She waited, tapping her fingers on the table.

She waited, with a pencil in her hands, drawing vague, round marks in the margins.

She waited sitting by the window. The horizon was flat until the mountains and behind the Seven Brothers stood a column of white clouds.

The cloud seemed, with its air of an ethereal cathedral, as if it would tell her something, but the idea remained balanced between consciousness and nothingness, an elusive specter. The caviar's effect was mild.

She returned to the can and quickly ingested the entire contents.

A saline reflux soured her throat. She swallowed several times and sat back from the table to examine her drafts once more, looking for an artistic idea for the community. She wanted to astonish, as with *Dream Time*. She wanted to achieve something that would be spoken about for months and months.

She looked back at the scribbles in the margins. Bubbles. Soap bubbles. Soap bubbles produced by a musical instrument ... her head had become heavy, she had to support it with one hand. Concentric bubbles whose convexities reflected different images, darting fish overlapping children playing ring-a-round the rosie; ducks crossing the boundaries between two worlds, cutting the spheres with the V-lines of their formations.

V for victory. *V* for victor. *V* for ...

Olì collapsed on the table. She opened her eyes for a moment without seeing anything, but her ears registered a faraway sound—like a cannon shot.

The drumming of thunder and the bright effects of lightning had accompanied the first roar, Impiastera had told her. The rock inhabitants had hastened to arrange tubs, pots, vats, and plastic bins on the bridges. Massimeh had collected enough water to be able to trade; at Castello's they had opened the hatches of underground cisterns; Impiastera had stripped and washed under the flood; Oja Mommìa, in hysterics, had fled to the top of the building, where he always kept a canoe ready for emergencies and had spent those hours shouting in horror, huddling in the life jacket, draining the boat with a bucket.

Upon awakening, Olì had found the plum leaves glossy and bright, the bridge washed, spotted with bright puddles.

Forty years with no rain. She had never seen a thunderstorm. The last one went back to a time when she was too small to remember. And she'd slept right through it.

"You are the only one who remembers. All those I know have come to me to have that day erased. They want eternal turquoise skies and eternal glorious suns. Impiastera, my neighbor, told me that the sky had descended and pressed on her head."

"The water from the sky was beautiful," whispered Tilde.

"Rain. Water that falls from the sky is called 'rain.'"

"Rainrainrain," sang the little girl to herself..

Olì turned the ball to get a better focus on the images that slid across the scratched wall of the apartment. The raindrops formed an irregular pattern along the bare walls.

"Well then, do you want to erase it?"

"No."

Tilde sat down, the sphere staying stuck in her navel but the fold of her belly deformed the image, rounding out the edges and merging land and sky.

"I don't want to."

"Your grandmother said ..."

"I don't care. I don't even know if she's really my grandmother. She and her friends pass the time fishing, painting fish mouths blue and throwing them back in the water."

This explained the fish with the blue muzzles that were sometimes caught in the nets.

"They grease the piers with coconut oil to laugh at people who slip off. They tangle the fishermen's nets and crucify gulls on the booms. Just because they are stupid, do I have to be stupid, too? I love rain. I'd love to see it again. They say that in the north, during certain times of the year …"

Delicately, Olì removed the sphere from Tilde's navel and rubbed it with a soft cloth.

"You'll have to laugh, too, when your grandmother and her friends do their tricks," she warned her. "Otherwise she'll know that I didn't take away your memory."

"I'm capable of pretending."

The little girl jumped down from the bed and started to look around the apartment, curious.

"What's that?"

She indicated the large fireplace covered in marble that occupied a corner of the living room.

"When it was cold on winter evenings, there was a fire in there, and everyone warmed up together, drank hot chocolate and mulled wine and threw mandarin peels into the flames to perfume the air."

The little girl touched the shelf, examined the hearth, put her head inside, and looked up toward the chimney.

"You can see the sky!"

Olì put the computer in a drawer and hastened to imitate her.

High above, very high, the black soot funnel of the chimney opened in a clear blue box.

The little girl had gone completely into the hearth and with monkey-like agility climbed along the funnel, resting her bare feet on the roughness inside.

"Come down. You could get hurt."

The annoyance at Tilde's invasion hardened her voice. After a moment of hesitation, the little girl descended. Her hands, her feet, her face, and swimsuit were black. And she left her footprints on the white wooden parquet.

"Look, I'm drawing a treasure map!"

The row of dark traces brought to mind the traced signs on the parchment of an old pirate.

"Look! It's treasure!" laughed Tilde, embracing the soft dummy, hidden behind the curtain.

"Oh, how soft!"

The little girl clutched the human form, which appeared to reciprocate, wrapping its arms around her and leaning its small head on Tilde's shaved skull.

"I'm here! I'm back!"

The grandmother had arrived just in time to claim her granddaughter. Olì received her payment and watched them leave. The sooty Tilde, aft, used all of her strength to wrap the elastic crank with a fake smile printed on her face while the old woman sat in the bow, chattering about her visions.

The presence of the little girl had really thrown her off balance. She was ashamed to feel relieved that they were gone. Was she becoming an oyster like the other residents?

Olì woke up in the middle of the night. The house creaked, the wind was rising. She got up and with a flashlight retraced Tilde's tracks on the floor. A shadow was crouched on the path, scrubbing the boards, puffing and muttering. It was using the computer sphere to clean, and when it turned, it had the face of a fish, the mouth twisted from one ear to the other, blue like the sky.

Olì woke up. It was dark. The house creaked, slammed by the wind. The feeling that something was going to happen gave her a strange excitement. She picked up the loose laundry, stiff, dried by the sun, and closed the window even though the air was muggy. Already in the past, the clash between the hot and cold winds had caused tornadoes and cyclones, but now a cold terror gripped her.

Out there in the darkness, a huge invisible animal stretched, expanding, taking possession of the air, the water, the fragile rock structure. A sudden blow like the breath that extinguishes a candle and stillness stopped every sound. Olì no longer heard the gentle lapping of the sea downstairs, the tinkling of the metal ropes that anchored the pier, the fluttering of the flag with the Quattro Mori on top of the corroded antenna.

And then the cold. An intense cold lay siege to the house, slipped under the door, breathed on the windowpanes, glazing them with an opaque material. Olì clutched the doll, tied it to her back, the arms knotted under her neck, the legs around her hips. A pleasant warmth spread through her body, restoring her courage, but the temperature continued to drop.

The house contracted, moaning under the wind's icy caress. Olì's teeth started chattering. She desperately searched in the drawers, remembered having seen, many years before, a woolen cap with earmuffs, there! A funny object, lemon yellow, with a pompom on top. If she put it under her chin and the heat expanded her thoughts, she could think straight.

She went downstairs and found that the water in the buckets in which she kept fish was hardened. She poured out the contents; the animals were locked in a tower of ice from which stuck out tails, fins, and some algae. At the bottom of the ladder, where the sea first lapped the marble, there was an irregular slab, dark blue. The doll's heat couldn't dissipate her fear.

And the small Sar with eight digits? Had he been able to take refuge in her den?

As the doll's head rose quickly up the stairs, the coconut broke off and rolled down a step, producing a sound dampened by the ski mask. Olì quickly disassembled her creation (feeling a small bit of regret for the soft creature), loosened the joints, got rid of the pressed wadding that formed the jacket, emptied the pants and woolen gloves of dried seaweed, and dressed herself. The thermal material seemed to activate upon contact with the skin. When she put the ski mask over the woolen cap, she felt a sense of protection like that exuded by ancient armor. In her database, she had a folder dedicated to "metal finishes." In some works the angels wore camisoles and iron leggings.

Her feet, used to sandals, didn't cope well with the rubber-soled boots, but she still tightened the laces.

She went upstairs, bringing the lobster bucket next. She was hungry, very hungry. She poured the contents into a pot, brought it to a simmer on an electric plate, and for the first time in her life, savored the lobsters boiled. She broke every claw and greedily sucked out its contents.

Refreshed by the food, she opened the door of the house, an armored frame on which she had welded some polycarbonate planks, and stuck her nose outside. The frost slapped her cheeks, clutched the tip of her nose in a vice. She immediately closed the door once more.

She assessed the few pieces of furniture in her apartment and finally decided on the basket in which she kept the linen, a kind of rectangular bamboo chest. She unscrewed the hinges on the cover, flattened the corners, and put it in the hearth. She tried to light it on fire. It didn't work. The lighter blackened the edge, but the braided fibers resisted. There must be a way. She consulted some antique paintings of tables, gathered in the "Fires" folder. *The Burning of the Houses of Lords and Commons* by Turner and *The Fire of Rome* didn't help. Nothing showed how the ancients ignited it.

While gazing at the pictures, something pinched her side. She put a hand in her pants, scratched, and pulled out a piece of dried algae. Pieces. She soon had a nice mound in the middle of the room. She put them in the fireplace and lit them. They burned immediately with a creeping smell of salt and the abyssal depths. Olì blew on it, and the tongues of fire reached the basket, which started to hiss and complain.

After some minutes the basket became a bonfire that stretched up to the chimney in a bold attempt to escape. The heat punched her in the face, intense as the sun at midday. Olì sat in front of the fireplace, trapped by the spell of the flames. So this was how they warmed up in the past. She only lacked the hot chocolate, a drink she had never tasted.

When the better part of the basket had turned into ashes, Olì stirred the fire with small wooden objects, stools, salad containers, statues of sea gods carved in times of boredom, using floating wood fragments that the sea had carried up to her rock.

Finally the sun peeped in through the condensation on the windows. Olì walked out of the door. The air was still sharp, but the light gave her courage.

She rubbed her eyes in disbelief. The sea had become a solid slab. The boat's counterweights were trapped in ice, and the refrigerator case was raised up almost as if the appliance wanted to straighten up, to return to its old purpose.

She admired the sycamore on top of the roof. The conical weave of the branches turned up to the sky, ready to pick up every little drop of moisture, had turned into a crystal nest supported by the icy column of the trunk. A sculpture full of magic.

She descended the outer ladder and reached out to touch the sea. Solid. As hard and compact as earth. She pressed it with the tip of her foot. The ice resisted. She beat her foot on that torquoise floor and perceived layers and layers under her soles.

She took a few steps with a pounding heart. She walked on water! She was walking on the sea! You could reach the other rocks by walking.

Feeling bold, she went faster, slipping and slamming her ass on the slab. The padding in her pants cushioned the blow, but her coccyx hurt. She stood up and began walking cautiously.

She headed for Impiastera's rock.

Her concern mounted with every step as she remembered that most of the houses had no windows. She came under her friend's pier, lowered the ski mask, and called to her loudly. Her breath crystallized and fell to the ground with a slight rattling sound.

No one responded. She climbed up the ladder and opened the door. Impiastera was in the hammock between two sunken poles, naked under a sheet, rigid like dried fish. The windows of the house were veiled by striped cotton curtains, and the hammock was placed in such a way that the current between the two openings flowed day and night. A great strategy to deal with heat, a bad idea with the cold.

Over the table shone five plates sugared with frost, each one containing the same fish-shaped dessert, and for sure every sweet was a variant of the recipe that her friend was studying. Everything inside was covered with a frosty coat.

Two tears rolled down Oli's cheeks and immediately changed into glass sticks. She pulled them out of her eyes because she couldn't blink.

The fear of being left alone, of being the only survivor, made her flee. She had to find out if the others had left her.

She started to run toward the hospital, stumbled, but managed to regain her balance. She began to walk with exasperating slowness.

"Everything is fine! God protected me!"

Massimeh waved his arms and leaned out of an upper window. From the terrace above his head shimmered the helicopter's tail, the original red faded into rose like a giant frozen shrimp.

"I woke up during the night and heard the voice of an

angel. It said: 'Massimeh, arise and cover yourself!' I grabbed all the blankets I could find, but they weren't enough. I was shaking. Then I went down into Intensive Care and looked for a drug to help me."

"And did you find it?" asked Olì, happy to be able to speak with another human being.

"God knew what would happen and had anticipated that I'd need it."

He showed her some disposable syringes sealed in plastic envelopes, filled with a yellowish liquid, and soon after Olì heard him come bustling down the stairs. Massimeh dragged a stretcher piled high with thin, shiny blankets.

"I'm coming with you. I must bring God's salvation to everyone."

Since the helicopter had stopped, he welcomed the faithful to the hospital's great rock but avoided moving himself. The ice was changing things.

The preacher wore a plain garment made out of blankets. Olì felt a sleeve.

"It's too thin."

"But hot, very hot! I sewed it this evening with a no. 3 saturated wire. God inspired me."

He threw one of those sheets on her, and within a few seconds Olì felt an intense heat. It had to be a special yarn, which collected the solar rays and used them to generate heat.

Slipping on the ice, Massimeh kneeled over the stretcher, pushing it with an IV pole. Olì sat at the other end. The rubber wheels advanced without slipping.

First they headed toward the rooftops populated by clams and mussels.

The wires between the walls looked like the lines in a notebook drawn on the white sheet of the ice. The black shells of mussels were dreary words, incomprehensible. Olì knocked on the door of a terrace, and Monia opened it a crack. Teeth chattering, wrapped in a cotton jersey, a sarong around her head, her face and hands bruised.

"You okay?"

"We're alive. We closed the windows in time and burned the mussel rope to heat up."

From the house came the strong smell of roasted seafood.

They left three blankets, a blessing, and continued on.

Tzugata's rock threatened the worst. His apartment had a roof supported by four pillars. On the rooftop terrace grew date palms, the fronds paralyzed in the dry air like large green stars.

They went around the house between cat statuettes and ragged cushions, calling to him loudly. The answer came from a small screen inserted into a wall.

"What do you want, pests?"

"Tzugata, where are you?"

"In a safe place. What do you want?"

Olì approached the screen. It was a closed circuit monitor and showed the corpulent owner of the house soaking in a hot tub. The temperature of the water, judging by the rising steam, had to be like a broth.

Olì felt stupid. She should have known that a rich man like Tzugata had a refuge to withstand any weather. Probably the surface apartment was only a facade, a hidden trapdoor leading to a lower floor equipped with every sort of comfort.

They went on their way.

A little farther down, they found a fisherman with a pickaxe. He shattered ice and collected it in plastic bags. Heavy rubber boots covered up to half of his thigh, but from there he wore only shorts and a t-shirt.

Massimeh threw one of God's blankets across his shoulders, but the man shook him off.

"I'm hot," he muttered.

"You're tiring your heart," the preacher replied. "You need to get warm."

"Go away, you make me waste time."

And with even more decisive blows he sprayed fragments in every direction.

"I need ice. I need to conserve fish."

"The fish are frozen now," said Olì.

The fisherman kept mumbling between filling the buckets.

When Massimeh insisted that he at least accept a blanket, he looked at him like he was crazy and threatened him with the pickaxe.

"It's hard to do good," the preacher commented.

An explosion made them turn toward the rock of Monte Claro.

Halfway there was Oja Mommìa's rock. He was displaying a sheet that was partitioned into four sections; on two quadrants were painted white towers, and on the other two the curve of a gigantic wave crossed with an "X."

Mommìa, clothed in a black and yellow wetsuit, was skipping happily among the sycamores.

"You're done!" he shouted at the frozen sea. "We beat you! You can't do anything anymore!"

And he smashed the little frozen crests of the waves with the depth meter tip.

Another explosion, and blossoming in the sky were red and green fireworks.

"Hurrah! Hurrah!" shouted Oja.

At the height of the tumbledown cocoon they called the Library, a group of ancients pierced the ice with electric battery rods and dropped in fireworks as large as sticks of dynamite. Covered with synthetic fur, their faces were painted red, black, and white; they danced in a circle, making a racket with their anklets to drums beaten by trembling girls and boys.

"Today it's hot, eh!" a man painted partially red shouted, euphorically. With a kind of large gun, he fired rockets in the air, which burst a few meters from the ground, falling in the form of gold and silver confetti. The old ones danced joyfully in the sparking swirl, and the drummers were crying from the cold without stopping their pounding, looking for some heat in the convulsive rhythm of their arms.

Olì recognized Tilde's grandmother in the group, her face painted blue. She was dancing ring-a-round the rosie with her comrades, frantically moving her feet. Her group was wearing fish-shaped masks, thin transparent plastic gills stretched over wooden slats, pointed fins on their backs.

"Today it's hot, eh!"

The dance sped up. The old ones wore heavy mountain climbing boots, but their legs were bare, covered with varicose veins reddened by the cold.

Olì moved on to search for Tilde. She wasn't among the drummers. She searched within the library walls that emerged from the ice, covered in barnacles and algae blackened by the low temperature. She found her crouched beneath a sloping roof trimmed in thin opaque icicles, wearing only a bathing suit, a drum abandoned at her feet. She crawled up to her and wrapped her in two hospital blankets. Tilde didn't even notice, paralyzed with her forehead against her knees, with bluish nails and skin. She massaged her back and arms. Tilde was already rigid! Perhaps the heart had surrendered and she was trying to resuscitate a corpse, but after a few moments the little girl lifted her head and turned her gaze on that which had woken her.

A harder explosion than before showered them in icy crystals. The old ones exulted—a huge firecracker trapped in ice had opened a breach in the rigid expanse of the sea, and they immediately rushed to enlarge it with hot sticks, revealing the water underneath, dark and firm.

"Today it's hot, eh!"

"Let's take a bath!" a woman replied.

Without thinking twice the man dove toward the pit.

"Do it!" shouted another.

"It's like Poetto!"

Massimeh went from one to the other, trying to prevent them from plunging into the water, but they dodged him and rushed happily into the breach. Even Tilde's grandmother followed the group of divers, waving a fan of colored scales. A few seconds after touching the water, the smiles turned into contracted grins. The old ones, demented, fell silent in the glassy obscurity, arms at their sides, their bodies numb from sudden freezing, without a groan.

Those who had remained dry, after a moment of uncertainty, burst into silly laughter.

Massimeh had seized a man half immersed and tried to remove him from the packed ice.

"Help me!" he shouted.

The others continued to shoot off firecrackers, dance, and shake their anklets. The drum players had stopped, uncertain, but with a pinch on the neck, the old ones made them continue. Olì carried Tilde to the stretcher and covered her with all the remaining blankets.

Massimeh had succeeded in dragging the man out to dry and aimed a syringe at his neck.

"The heart, in the heart," Olì suggested.

The preacher pierced his chest and pushed in the plunger.

After some seconds the old one coughed, lifted his chest, and took a deep breath.

"God is great."

Massimeh raised his eyes and hands to the sky, but a moment later the old one unsteadily threw himself back into the chilly water.

Olì decided that she had had enough of idiots and idiocy. She made the kids stop playing and wrapped them in blankets.

The old ones tried to stop her, wanting more music, more dancing, more casks. Olì responded by hitting them with the drumsticks; a woman tried to bite her arm, and Massimeh had to detach her.

The arrival of the municipal motor boats broke up the festive group.

The boats were hoisted onto wheeled carts tugged by small crawlers. Olì recognized Elis in the cloaked figure in the bow. The crew came down and made the kids drink hot fil'e ferru diluted with water before getting them on board. Olì was curious to see how they would convince those crazy people to cover up, but the rescue team just sprayed them with a frothy foam. It stuck to the skin and developed a pleasant warmth, isolating the body, while they were still wiggling and dancing.

They'd been around since dawn, Elis explained. The apartments on Cadello's, Armi's, and the Students' rocks didn't have windows. The inhabitants had died of cold, struck down in their hammocks while they slept. But the small family that lived on Magistero's rock were saved, thanks to the habit of keeping the north-facing windows closed to counter the waves due to the speed of the boats.

She knew from the radio that her colleagues had found other survivors on the Cep atoll and the Quartiere del Sole.

Massimeh asked the counselor to take him with them. The stretcher was too heavy to push; Olì demanded a drum, put Tilde on it, and dragged her to the ice by pulling her with the straps that the players had hung around her neck.

"Back to my rock."

"How did you lose your leg?"

Murena lifted his left leg: from the knee to the foot was smooth, white, completely synthetic; the insertion of the kneecap disappeared into the short, fringed trousers.

"Nice, huh?" he said, knocking on it with his knuckles. "A shark attacked me while I was fishing. It's a story to tell the grandkids."

"Tell me the truth."

Murena looked around, cautious. An unnecessary precaution because they were the only souls on Olì's rock.

"Look here, I'll tell you because you're like a doctor. When there was the Great Frost, I made a bet with a neighbor over who could stay longer in cold water."

Olì nodded. She had heard every sort of harebrained story over the last few days while the ice melted and the sea became navigable again.

"I won the bet, but the leg was black and they had to cut it off."

"I'm sorry, Murena, I don't do memory embellishments anymore."

"What does that mean?"

"It means you'll remember the bet."

"But I want to forget. I also want you to erase the memory of the Great Frost. That Curcaio bastard was able to fill an ice store and now sells frozen fish he passes off as fresh. That too I want to forget."

"I've decided that remembering is better than forgetting."

"I'll give you a box of lobsters."

"Frozen, I imagine. No thanks."

"Two boxes."

"You're lucky, Murena. The leg reminds you always of the Great Frost, the day on which you could walk on water. That's a story to tell the grandkids."

Murena started toward the door with a resentful haughtiness. He turned at the threshold.

"I could say that during the Frost we had nothing to eat, and I cut off my leg to roast it!"

"Perfect."

The fisherman went out, swollen with renewed pride.

Olì returned to the table on which were scattered the elements of her new artistic work: the cold binoculars. Using fragments of glass honed by the sea, she had reproduced the reflections of the sunlight on the ice. By rotating the eyepiece ring, one could observe a maritime landscape that slowly changed, the colors moving from blue to gray; dark clouds taking possession of the sky, the sea wrinkling, the waves raging. Tilde had suggested that she insert a rumble of thunder, and so, from a small side microphone, it could also have sound effects exactly as the child remembered them. The grumbling of the thunder gave way to a crescendo of wind that froze the sea, producing a shrill crystal sound that Olì had kept in her memory from that night.

The frosty effect was intensified by the insertion in the eyepieces of some menthol crystals that made the eyes tear up when the binoculars were put on the nose.

Persistence of Memory was the name of her new artistic project.

Copied from Dalí, but no one would ever know. The commune had commissioned a hundred cold binoculars; they had paid for it with fruit and items to barter.

"Olì!"

She looked at the dock. Tilde was standing on a surfboard, the oar in front of her.

"It's all ready."

Olì looked to the west. The sun had almost disappeared on the other side of the mountains. The sea reflected the violet sky streaked with red and gold. Small, irregular icebergs broke the monotony of the water's expanse. A great number of boats were waiting, heading eastward, a few meters from her rock. Every raft, piece of wood, or surfboard hosted at least two citizens. On communal motorboats were arranged the whole city council.

Before leaving the house Olì slipped into a jacket and pants. The air was still biting. She sat on Tilde's surfboard and was escorted to Impiastera's rock.

Her friend's body was stretched out in a canoe, soaked in oil, and covered with red hibiscus flowers.

With wide and solemn gestures so that everyone could see, Olì lit a soaked wooden torch and placed it on Impiastera's chest. She then cut the mooring, and the canoe slid toward the sunset. She had carefully calculated the current and wind direction. The pyre rose slowly and rivaled the flames of the sky.

The boat stood out against the dark backdrop of the mountains, an island of fire between islands of ice, in the deep calm of sunset. Tilde blew into a shell and a sad bellow went through the neighborhood, a note long and deep announcing the end, predicting the end, accompanying the end.

Many years later, the citizens still remembered that day, a moment in their hard, mundane existence in which life, color, scents, heat, cold, air, and water were fused in a work in which they themselves had been a part.

GABOLA

Knock knock knock.

Furao worked the chisel carefully, without losing his rhythm or light touch. Prangi appreciated that expert hand, especially at night, when a leaden solemnity fell on Little Tuvu and a sneeze sounded like a clanging bell.

Knock knock knock.

Limestone fragments accumulated under the excavation area. Prangi removed them with a short shovel, throwing them onto the floor of the access shaft. The fresh air of the spring night came in through the quadrangular opening of the tomb, and the work proceeded at a good pace. The perfect time to dig.

The noise of a sudden collapse announced that the partition had yielded, and they could access the next tomb. Furao put the tools into his belt and slipped through the cavity with the twist of an eel. Prangi followed him, struggling a bit to get his hips to pass through the opening.

"You could enlarge it," he protested.

"Eat less pasta," Furao grinned.

The band of glow-in-the-dark fabric they wore around their heads emitted a blue light, making them look like saints with halos. The light was dim but enough to make out the body covered with red ocher lying on its back, surrounded by terracotta pots and bronze objects. Gold chains and glass paste pendants glittered on his chest.

Furao jumped over the body and leaned toward the opposite wall, resuming his chiseling. Sometimes, in one night, they were able to break into five tombs in quick succession.

Prangi started bagging the pots, but when he reached for the jewels, he stopped, frightened. The corpse's head, dry and shrunken, reminded him of his first child, dead some months after being born. Eventually, the old and newborns look alike. And the tombs of Little Tuvu are the cradles of the ancestors. Life is a circle—like a snake with its tail in its mouth, which he had seen carved at the entrance to the mortuary.

Tears crowded on the edge of his eyelashes, the dam yielded, and Prangi tried to stem the flood by burying his face in his left arm. The right was busy grabbing the necklaces, earrings, and bracelets, and throwing them in the bag.

Four tombs later, Prangi and Furao went up the shaft of the last tomb, keeping to the notches carved along the walls, the tied bags on their backs. The hill was shrouded in darkness. One always went to Little Tuvu on moonless nights. A damp breeze caressed the grass, which, in some places, reached the chests of the two skinny figures walking down the slope. The halo radiated by the luminous bands enlarged their heads. If an insomniac living in the buildings that surrounded the hill had appeared at that moment, he would have believed that aliens had landed on Little Tuvu.

The artifacts were lined up on Famida's table, where she examined them in the usual way, meticulously, holding a large jeweler's lens to her right eye. She reviewed every vessel, every brooch, every pendant, without making a comment or a sound. At moments it seemed like she wasn't even breathing.

Furao walked around her restlessly muttering, *C'mon ... how long does it take? ... still? ...*

"Sit down!" demanded Prangi. "You look like a hungry cat."

Furao perched the edge of his ass on a chair but was on his feet a moment later.

"Admit it! It's fabulous stuff! The best we've ever brought you."

Famida let the lens slip down her cheek and caught it with one hand. She backed away in from the table in her wheelchair and half turned on the wheels, looking first at Prangi and then at Furao.

"Yes, it's beautiful. But it's *gabola*."

Gabola opened the fridge. A whiff of something rotten nearly knocked him over, still foggy from sleep. The vegetables were melted into a brown mush, and the minestrone, prepared with such care just three days earlier, bubbled like a stygian swamp.

The solar panels were out of order. Curse Cresia's silver tongue. The best panels in the city. I'll give you the panels. I'd like to strangle you with them, really.

Now I have to feed everything to the compost. Double curses.

The hydrolates! Ten bottles of rose juice, ten hard-earned bottles, and maybe they're now rotten water. Something is moving. What is it? A caterpillar. Excuse me, Mr. Caterpillar, if I busted up your paradise. What are you doing? Romancing the perfumed drops beaded at the sides of the glass neck of the bottles. Look at this bug. It's a bug, and it understands everything. He knows where to go. Fine, man, you've earned your way into paradise. Now I'll take you to the garden and leave you on one of my gallica officinalis. Looks like you're galloping on the rose. It must be nice to rub all those ugly green hairs on a smooth, fresh petal. Surely afterwards it feels smooth and fresh. And fragrant. It must be nice to dive into the heart of the perfume.

Everyone needs a small amount that makes them feel at peace. Because there is a war out there, but here there's peace. Now I sit on the wall and take my dose of peace, and then I can jump into the middle of the war among the madmen.

Look how serene the air is. And the roofs of the buildings below Little Tuvu soon to be springboards ready to launch you up to where the sky is bluer, above the turquoise glass of the Lagoon. And I can run straight to the jagged black of the mountains, but before I reach them I turn left, skipping the tightrope of the road that separates the pond from the sea and fly close to the waves. I could escape from the island, go to the continent.

Did I say "escape"? A silly idea. Gabola, how do certain thoughts come to you? Such nonsense. Come back down, come back. Stay on Little Tuvu, your peace.

Look at how soft the grass is that bends to the wind ... wait, wait, there's something strange over there. Shit. Another visit from the saints. I go back home and grab the big flashlight I always keep ready on a shelf, and I walk quickly between the asphodels and the thistles.

The crushed stems lead to the tombs in the southeastern sector.

Oh, I gasp. I've already replaced the funeral goods throughout that sector. As I climb the slope, I imagine the saints' faces after the dealer tells them that they've brought back useless copies. A loquat tree gives me its fruit, small and a bit stale. Thanks, tree, it's very sweet.

I jump the wall and sit at the lathe, sucking my fingers. Yesterday evening I stopped halfway through working on a terracotta perfume jar. I remove the damp cloth that covers the raw material and compare it with the original: the neck must be lengthened and the lip of the jar tightened. With a vigorous kick-start the lathe and pot begin to turn.

The eternal spiral turns and turns, my thoughts are spinning, growing thin like a spider's web, and I'm weaving myself in my own joy. Even the laboratory turns on an invisible pin, always the same and always different. The map of Little Tuvu that I painted hangs on the opposite wall, red numbers for the tombs still to be visited, black numbers for those already done, question marks for unexplored areas.

Friends ask me: *Gabola, why do you waste time remaking ruins? What's up with you?* Nothing comes to me. Not everything is done for money. Things are done because they have to be done. And I do them.

With the flick of an elbow, I put the round table in motion on which I've laid the funeral equipment of tomb number 79. Useful, this table. Uncle Wu gave it to me after he closed the restaurant and opened the gambling house. I put the jars on it, the jewelry, the perfume bottles, the bowls, all that I have to reproduce. Every day I run it and move on to the next piece. Order and method—the secret of every well-done task.

The splashes of clay on the floor seem like sparrow droppings. The glass beads around the crucible are dragonfly tears. The electric stove is off, no glassy paste until I replace those stupid panels. That thief, Cresia. The washing machine! I set it last night; it must have stopped, too! I'd like to see you hang from the gallows.

I wet my fingers again and finish smoothing out the perfume bottles. There, equal to the original. The Punic potter who made it would be proud of me. I block the lathe and check at what point I am with the copies. I've reproduced almost all of the artifacts of tomb number 79, but no power, no cooking. Oh, Cresia, I'll take you by the neck and make you sweat my money. And then I'll collect it with a teardrop vial.

I go see what I can find out about the condition of the washing machine. Sheets as dry as a desert. And already the well pump is connected to the fabulous solar panels.

I resign myself to using the manual pump. Grandma had installed it after winning the lottery. The winnings had gone to her head, and she also had part of the roof redone. Thanks,

Granny; at least I can sleep dry. I fill a couple of buckets and immerse the sheets in the cement sink. Without detergent. Detergent pollutes and ruins fabrics. And then they're still almost clean. I do laundry once a month!

At midday the Lagoon shopping center is in full swing. Shops compete for attention. Steam rises from the frying food in the stalls. Fish, vegetables, and potato chips everywhere. The juice dispensers squeeze a quintal of Muraverax oranges every half hour. Exhibitors of ready-made clothes move on wheels and block your way, saying in a metallic voice, "Try me! Only three erui a piece!"

And there are still people who do it. But what do you feel, fool, that all are the same, size XXL, made on the continent in nondescript factories. Nothing, some fool always gets taken in. Buying is easy, just grab what you need and the seller's scanner sucks money from the credit card hanging around your neck. Then put your purchase in the cart that, since you entered, has followed you everywhere like a dog after a bone.

I, too, have my shadow on wheels. Poor cart; it will remain empty and waste energy unnecessarily. I never buy anything. Except that time I bought those solar panels, Cresia, that son of a bitch.

Here's his shop; the sign reads, *Sun In Your Eyes*. Now I'll give it to you, sun. In your eyes I'll give it to you. I start on the double but someone pulls me by my sleeve.

"Want urchins?"

Monzitta leans out from his bench loaded with thorny and shiny sea urchins sprayed with sea water.

"Later, Monzì. I have to get reimbursed by Cresia."

"Wait a minute. 'Cresia' and 'repayment' are opposites."

"Antithetical," corrects Marigosa, without lifting her eyes from her sewing machine.

"The concept holds," Monzitta replies. "Forget it, Gabola. Cresia will cheat you again."

"But no, now I can explain the problem ..."

"You can't explain anything to Cresia," Marigosa replies.

"He tells you what you need. And then he sells it to you!" Monzitta concludes.

I extricate myself and pass the threshold of *Sun in Your Eyes*, followed by my trusty cart.

"Do you think he can do it?" asks Monzitta.

Marigosa shakes her head.

"Cresia might have a guilty conscience ..."

"Which conscience is that?" grunts Marigosa, nervously tearing a thread from the edge of some pants.

Tripping over his trousers, a man stops in front of her and stares greedily at the sewing machine.

"Excuse me, how much to shorten a suit?"

Marigosa checks him out with an expert eye.

"Jacket twenty, pants ten."

The customer shudders. Then he sees the writing on the sign hanging on a coat rack: *Pay in Installments*.

"The minimum payment is ten erui per week," Marigosa forewarns him.

"Ugh, too expensive!"

"I eat every day, just like you," Marigosa replies, carefully folding the trousers she just finished.

The man glances at the urchin counter with little interest and then slips quietly away.

Monzitta keeps staring at the entrance to *Sun in Your Eyes*.

"There he is! He's leaving. And he's completely, absolutely ..."

A tower of plastic material protrudes from the cart behind Gabola, equipped with a four-petal propeller.

"... screwed."

"Men," mutters Marigosa. "All bark and no bite."

***

I return to my friends, satisfied and happy.

"See? I explained to him that solar panels at night are useless and Cresia solved the problem. He sold me a windmill, which supplies current during the night."

"For the modest sum of ...?"

"Oh, we made an exchange. I gave him three of my best jars decorated with red chevrons. Authentic faux high Neolithic."

"And when he realizes that they're fakes?" Monzitta blurts out. "He'll send the cops after you."

I move quickly three times, pretending to dodge an invisible object and laughing. Marigosa and Monzitta exchange a look. They know something I don't know, but today bad news can keep its distance.

"Want urchins?" Monzitta repeats.

"Mussels, lemons, and frozen vermentino."

I sit at a plastic table and set up the chair so as to see the gleam of the sun on the transparent floor. The shopping center covers the whole pond, and from some holes in the floor emerge islets of reeds and tufts of pink salicornia that are reflected in the glass walls and the ceiling. It's like being outdoors. Resembles the real peacefulness of Little Tuvu. A dose of artificial peace.

"Monzì, for you, is peace always artificial?"

He throws me a disgusted look.

"Shut up and eat."

A tray of half shells comes to me in which the raw muscles palpitate a dazzling orange. The color of the day. Breakfast of loquats, lunch of mussels. I'm hungry. The bread is made from durum wheat, and the wine is just grapes. Monzitta cares about tradition. I make the last drop disappear from the bottom of the glass and let myself float peacefully. The sun warms my legs. In the distance I can see the pyramids of salt—snowy, dazzling—and the big wind towers of the industrial area. The salt is an artistic installation by Arvo Finnico but from a distance it looks real, looks beautiful.

I stretch and get to my feet. Time to get to work.

"Monzitta, two pounds of special urchins."

He winks at me and from a tub under the bench, transfers about twenty urchins into a wicker basket. He gives me the basket, and I go to bring knowledge to the people.

"Cross stitch, petit point, hemstitch, grass stitch ..."

I approach two beautiful ladies standing in front of the showcase of filet lace and embroidered tablecloths. The women wear industrial clothes, but well-suited to their figures, so I know they can pay a seamstress. And if they can afford a seamstress, they might want to indulge other whims.

"I have any stitch you want. Also knitting, if you prefer that. German, English, shaven, grain of rice ..."

"I've always wanted to know how to knit," one of them sighs.

"Fifty erui, a couple of seconds of her time, and she'll make all the sweaters and scarves she wants for herself."

The woman looks to her friend for advice.

"I once bought the ability to make sushi."

"Ah, I sold it to her! Last year I purchased a batch of gastronomic skills. I hope she was satisfied."

"My husband loved it so much."

"But these abilities," the aspiring knitter intervened, "aren't they exhausted after a short amount of time?"

"My husband is dead, too," her friend shrugs.

"Oh, I'm sorry," I say.

"The sushi sat on my stomach."

"Do you also accept credit cards?"

"Naturally."

I unsheathe my portable reader, which is in the form of a Phoenician mask, a perfect Gabola brand reproduction, into which I insert the chip. I keep it hanging around my neck but hidden inside my shirt.

"What should I do?" asks the lady, lost.

"Eat."

I choose a violet urchin from the basket, cut the top off with scissors, uncover it, rinse off the entrails, and offer it to her. The lady swallows the eggs, slow and suspicious.

"Can I knit now? I have nothing in my head."

"It's not in your head. It's here." I raise my hands.

The friend is enjoying herself at her friend's expense. She enters the store, buys knitting needles and wool, the first she finds, and puts them in her friend's hand.

"Here, try. A nice sweater in rice stitch."

Look at how indecisive the customer is. And how, after holding the needles, she binds the yarn expertly, building the stitches.

Her hands work quickly; in less than a minute she's knitted three inches of rice-stitched wool.

Look at how she smiles and continues clicking the needles, unable to stop. Now she believes in miracles.

Payment, thank you, and then I leave.

A man stumbling over his long trousers approaches me; he keeps rolling up the sleeves of his baggy sweatshirt.

"Hey, man! Hey! Do you sell the skill to cut and sew fabric?"

I shake my head.

"I'd pay you well. Thirty erui!"

"Tailors and seamstresses prefer to take it to their graves."

He gestures irritably, and I carry on with my search for clients.

Two aspiring musicians point toward the saxophones in a display case. I cut through the crowd and reach them with my basket under my arm. I'm the Little Red Riding Hood of the Lagoon.

"Blues, jazz, rock, choose a style and you'll be able to play the saxophone better than John Coltrane."

"We were really looking for a birthday present for our daughter," one of them replies.

"Nothing better! Kids love to have a skill without the labor involved."

"It's illegal," mutters the other.

"All beautiful things are illegal."

They laugh and then ask me my price. Musical skills will cost extra. In addition to the manual ability to play an instrument, you must know how to read all the goat droppings along the staves, and the keys, and the breaks, and the accents; in conclusion, in my opinion, seventy erui would be the minimum.

The two don't even bat an eye. I offer a small black urchin, shiny like the vinyl of an ancient record. Since it's a gift, I pack it in an inflatable glass jar filled with salt water. The laughing mouth of the Phoenician mask sucks up the money from the credit card hanging around one of their necks. Thanks and see ya later.

The day goes well. I sell the ability to quickly learn Chinese and Arabic, the ability to make plants grow and thrive, and two abilities to write romance novels. The capacity to write is a small request; almost nobody reads long, complex stories. In fact, professional writers have become extinct, but perhaps the market is recovering.

I return to Monzitta and Marigosa. To my trusty urchin supplier I must give a percentage of my profits. I'm at the counter when an electronic sandwich board with flamingo legs jumps out at me.

Little Tuvu
Big House

screams the writing on the light board in myopia-proof print.

I stop, amazed. The flamingo senses my interest, comes up to me, and the ad keeps scrolling:

Apartments so modern so elegant so panoramic.
Building next on Little Tuvu
For reservations, call 070456111.

"How is this possible?" I exclaim.

"*Do you want to know more?*" the sign croaks. "*Give us a call!*"

While standing on one leg, it stretches a disposable phone out to me with the other in which the number to call is stored. I'm about to take it when a fat guy in ill-fitting clothes trips on his pants and lands on the flamingo, smashing it into a mess of pink feathers, plastic fragments, and bright letters. The telephone flies into a vat full of urchins and sinks into the water.

The fat guy's friends cackle; Monzitta threatens them with her fists.

"Get outta here, you devil! I'll give you a knock you'll remember until New Years!"

He draws out the scraps of the phone with a fishing net while the overweight guy flees, holding up his pants with both hands.

I hear a ringing in my ears.

"What's all this about apartments on Little Tuvu?"

They glance at each other again.

"You know that residential development ..." Marigosa mentions, inserting a new spool.

"So? I've heard about it since I was a kid."

"It's been approved."

"Impossible. You can't build on Little Tuvu. It belongs to the city."

"Yeah, and I'm the Queen of England. You worried it'll ruin your income?"

The word "worried," in Monzitta's mouth, has four "r"s.

"I can find a place as a custodian wherever I wish. But the tombs? How do you build on the tombs?"

"Such clutter," Monzitta spits. "Modernity advances."

53

"With a steamroller," adds Marigosa. "I heard they're putting up eight-story buildings. With attics. Refined stuff, for the rich."

"Great. Wonderful. More work for us," the urchin dealer approves.

"How foolish. When will a rich man come here to eat your urchins?" Marigosa rebuts. "They go to the Buccaneer, who buys the shells in Mexico and makes eggs grow inside them with synthetic DNA."

I leave them still bickering and escape from the Lagoon. I need information. The bridges are crowded with people headed in the opposite direction, all with credit cards hanging around their necks and trusty carts close by. In the Avenue I find Palo chatting with Furao and Prangi, his right hand tightly holding the pole of a *No Parking* sign.

The two saints are pretty messed up; Furao has his arm in a sling and a gash running down his right cheek from temple to chin. Prangi's got three fingers of his right hand in plaster and a purple eye. Hey, Famida's touchy; if you try to sell her fake finds, she'll tan your hide with her Praetorians.

"Oh, Palo, you know anything about the buildings on Little Tuvu?"

"Gabola, you're behind the times. I know everything. They start building in two months."

"How is this possible? It's crazy!"

"Hey, if they're doing it, obviously they *can*." He switches hands on the pole.

"Little Tuvu isn't yours," argues Furao with a voice that's darker than tobacco.

"And the necropolis?"

"Some holes in the ground. Fill 'em and go," shrugs Palo.

The past means nothing to them.

"And history, our origins?"

"Origins? You, Prangi, where are you from?"

"From my mother's cunt."

Listen to them laugh, the sons of bitches. I cross the street and take the stairs to the cement factory, then I climb onto the roof of a building that leans against the rock of the hill and from here jump into the wreck of Villa Mura. I walk among the broken bricks and shattered tiles, on cardboard and old blankets, which shift, complain, and curse as I walk. Excuse me, it's a serious question.

Along the edge of the Catino I see from afar a figure totally in gray. It moves slowly and occasionally bends over to pick up something from the ground.

"Counselor!"

I start running and reach him in a few steps.

"Good afternoon, Gabola. I see you're out of breath."

Counselor Mossa-Sguincio is always well-groomed and the crease of his trousers as straight as the law.

"Counselor, you know they're building here on Little Tuvu?"

He collects two more asparagus. In his left hand he has a nice bunch. He says that they're tastier when he picks them himself.

"Of course I know it. I drew up the land sale contracts myself and the sale by the municipality."

I'm stunned. Then I see that a big, beautiful asparagus has escaped the lawyer's sharp eye, and the last thing I'm going to do is point it out; I'd rather lose my fingers.

"Gates, driveways, paved courtyards. Millennial olive trees in flowerbeds two meters by two meters. Where will you find asparagus, Counselor? And the chicory in spring? And chard in winter? You have to let me speak to the builder."

"Giuseppe Perdalonga only listens to what interests him. Do you have something to trade with him?"

And here he stops as if his tongue's dried up. He takes my arm.

"Gabola, you need to find a skill to sell."

***

"I see your ten and raise you twenty."

Look how the table is petrified. Everyone stares at me warily, even Sàtera, standing behind the dealer. When I joined the morning poker session, I was their student; now the teacher would like to skin me alive.

"The maximum bet is ten eruo cents," says the dealer, the mother goddess incarnate.

"I know what the limit is," I reply. "So, are you in or not?"

The other players fidget; those who have a good hand are tempted, the cowards disconsolately contemplate their two pair. Everyone's sweating, though the house is a room without a roof with walls covered in ivy.

Sàtera makes them stand up with a wave of her hand and sits in the dealer's place. A duel! I'm so happy I could dance.

"I see your twenty," the great poker player begins, throwing a banknote into the pot. "And I raise you a zero."

In her hands materialize two one hundred erui banknotes. I didn't believe they still existed. It's paper-money, plasticless people who live on Little Tuvu.

"Nice recovery. Here's my card. I guarantee that covers the amount."

"Invisible money," Sàtera comments contemptuously. She raises a finger, and one of the students brings a credit card reader. She directs the device scanner at my Phoenician mask. Looks at the screen and nods.

"Plus another two hundred," I raise.

The students hold their breath. Sàtera remains impassive, without blinking.

"I put two more zeroes on it."

From under the table she pulls out a metal box and opens it. Wads of hundred erui banknotes ten inches high.

Hearts pounding. An absolute novelty. I've never had forty thousand erui, neither watermarked nor plastic. I put the cards down.

"I fold."

Very calmly, Sàtera collects the dish and also takes the four hundred from my card. Her disciples exult; someone gives me a mocking whistle.

"Be thankful, Gabola, guys," Sàtera says. "Today was your teacher and showed you that the bluff can be killed by money."

"And if you were wrong? If I had aces?"

Sàtera laughs.

"Sometimes you have to lose to win."

This is big.

The lesson is over. Sàtera sends everyone away, but I don't get up.

"For four hundred erui I can have your attention."

I tell her about Little Tuvu, of the work that's about to begin. Of the name Perdalonga, the famous player who stands up like a setting spaniel.

"Counselor Mossa-Sguincio told me that Perdalonga is a poker fanatic. He plays with his fellow builders, but there's a guy who cleans his pockets every time, a little manager who scrapes by doing renovations. Perdalonga hates to lose, and I'd like to propose an exchange."

She nods and stands up.

"You want to offer him an irresistible pot."

She climbs up a ramp of rubble with the agility of a lizard and exits via a window without further ado. I follow her on the treacherous branch of the fig tree inside the solar green of the ailanthus leaves amidst annoyed bees and grasshoppers as large as my hand. It's cooler now. Here on the island everything is exaggerated—too green, too blue, too hot or too cold, too much life or too much death.

At a certain point when the verdure becomes suffocating, we go out into a ruined room. The grass has eaten the floor, but here and there are little islands of precious tiles. Sàtera leaps over a ditch dug by the water and lands on a short track of dusty marble inside a low-ceilinged room carved into the rock.

"This was the bathroom."

I spread my arms and dive into the red and blue of the frescoes. The pregnant goblets of poppies are reproduced in orderly file, glasses upon glasses of oblivion alternate with snakes and geometric patterns. A Roman tomb. The arcosolia in the walls are the niches in which they placed the urns along with gifts for the silent aunt, Persephone.

The sarcophagi have been blunted, polished, lined with tiles internally, connected to drains and water pipes.

"I had furnished it little by little, choosing each piece of furniture, each object, based on my taste."

She shows me a chandelier that has remained miraculously hung from the ceiling of the ante-bathroom, a metal spaceship burnished by time. An unreachable swing that I've known since I was a child.

"Villa Mura was yours!"

"I lost it in poker thirty-five years ago. What an idiot, huh? I gambled away paradise."

I'm spun around like a pottery wheel. Something tells me to pay attention to what I'm about to do, but how can I if I don't yet know what that will be?

"I had a flush, but he had a straight," Sàtera continues. "A fraudulent straight. I discovered it a few years later, thanks to a tip. He had a camera installed at my back and saw what I saw. He wants to win. Always."

"Perdalonga."

"He took my home and let it die. See? Still dead."

And so here we are at the old enclosure.

Sàtera's nose is up, sitting on a low stool, and Monzitta drops two drops of special water into her nostrils.

"Traveling nanites," I say, winking.

"Dwarves?" The champion frowns. "You've put dwarves up my nose?"

58

"There are dwarves, and then there are nanites," Monzitta blurts out. "They're intelligent cells."

Sàtera grimaces.

"They taste like urchins. How disgusting!"

"Our Lady protect us! Urchins are a delicacy for connoisseurs, for superfine palates."

He's a good one, that Monzì. He started at age ten with a kit of Echidnas found by chance in some dude's bag. A distracted aunt who didn't notice he was taking it. Monzitta doesn't care about learning biology but understood how to develop cell cultures and now handles pipettes and slides better than a chemist.

"Now you have to play."

I brought with me a shiny new deck. I break the seal and start shuffling the cards, scattering them on the edge of a fragrant algae tank, wood embalmed from salt. The smell of a grandmother's sundresses enclosed in a closet. Under the water's surface the sharp eyes of the urchins look in every direction. In the next tub over, clams lie one on top of the other, pretending to be stones but in reality forming a rampart to escape.

Sàtera responds to the call of the cards with energetic nimbleness. Look at how well she cuts the twenty-eight cards, how she distributes them fluidly and confidently, a light breeze runs through her fingers and lines up suits and face cards in our hands. Expanding her range, she looks at them with the wooden face of a saint and patiently waits for me to open.

There's some bickering at the start because Monzitta would like to bet urchins, but she's opposed.

"It takes money, real money. No cash, no thrills."

Monzitta plays cautiously, but more than five cents at the opening. I make a dark bet of ten erui, just for laughs. Sàtera shakes her head.

"Fool!" Monzitta scolds me.

"I lose now, but then I'll win."

"Play with Perdalonga," Sàtera says, "and you'll know what it means to win and lose."

We change cards and relaunch amid gurgling siphons and the splutter of clams. Sàtera wins and takes away the pot with the same impassivity as when she started playing. Monzitta lost five erui and wants the champion to return it.

"It was a match for show."

"I never play for show."

Monzitta looks at me cross-eyed and curses the moment when he decided to help me. I have empty pockets, but the nanites have mapped all of the champion's neural connections. Soon the quintessence of her poker skills will drain from her body.

For the occasion I brought two authentic tear vials found in tomb number 19, the one with the snakes carved above the entrance, one of the first that I emptied of the originals and filled with my copies. Two opal glass amphorae that give off turquoise glints.

I put the vials near the outer corners of her eyes, black and deep like obsidian, and wait.

"Cry," I say.

"Why?"

"The nanites leave the brain by way of the optical nerve."

Sàtera blinks, squeezes her eyes shut.

"Keep going."

She presses her fingers on her eyes, dry like sandpaper.

"She has an enzymatic resistance to the irritating effects of the exiting nanites," Monzitta says.

"Shut up, Monzì," and then catching Sàtera's eye, "Think about Villa Mura. Remember how beautiful it was before, when the shiny white windows opened onto the panorama of the gulf. When the tile patterns were like fireworks. And water flowed from the taps instead of entering from the roof, and every morning you woke up among linen sheets, opening your eyes on the ceiling fresco."

The champion grimaces, her serene features give way, roll slowly downwards, channel upon channel of sad skin, ready to receive the flood of tears.

"I stopped crying for my house."

"Then remember how that son of a bitch took it away from you," Monzitta bursts out. "Manulonga, they had to call him! He was already rich, had no need for Villa Mura, and he took it by deception! With an old trick: a camcorder and an accomplice who told him what to play!"

Sàtera's face lights up like a match. Her cheeks swell, sparks jump from her eyes, her teeth jut out of her mouth. A storm of insults spills over on the builder, but no tears.

I sit on the floor.

It's a bad situation. I need to recover the nanites within twenty minutes, otherwise her antibodies will destroy them and Little Tuvu will be turned into a camel hump loaded with eight-story boxes. Lost, lost forev ...

"Sàtera, sometimes you have to lose to win," I tell her point blank.

"Oh, little one, whom do you take me for? I taught you that."

"You're playing your greatest game. It's your moment. No bluffs. You have a straight flush, and you play everything. All your skills! After that, you won't be able to play poker anymore. Never again."

She stares at me stunned for a few seconds, blinking and already at the second blink the tears flow, silent, inexorable.

The Tuvu hill is fenced in but has three known—and many unknown—points of access. All invariably inconvenient.

Marigosa goes over the gate, which is next to a cave. The cave, closed in by a modern tilting door, opens only to house the cars of engineer Fois and his sons, who live in the opposite villa. She falls to the ground on the other side and recovers the package that she pushed between the bars. She takes one of the thousand paths impressed in the grass, keeping her eyes down, attentive to wells and pits. That place is full of booby traps, and she fell into the biggest one of all, the trap named "Gabola." One autumn day, one of those days in which the lead of the sky handcuffs the wrists of those who work on the Earth, while she was sewing the border of a jacket, she had seen Gabola arrive at the Lagoon with his hair wet from the rain. In passing by, he had smiled at her. The distant rumbling of the impending storm had been the soundtrack, and her needle had gone awry.

Around Gabola she always feels a bit bad humored, as if his presence gave her an irritated stomach. And as she climbs up the hill, she stomps on the ground, trampling wild orchids and cetonia.

The empty fountain basins announce the house. Marigosa crosses the orchard and looks up. The ancient villa stands fragile and sharp among the pines. In the first patio the wind shakes three sheets spread out to dry on the wire, good old linen worn by many washings. On the other she finds Gabola. He's shaving in front of a mirror hanging from a tree branch. He rinses the razor in a black lekythos painted with human and animal figures.

"Is Cresia's powered windmill at a standstill?"

"The blades turn," he answers, twisting his mouth to pass the blade over his lip. "But no current."

"Cheating the cheater."

"I'll be connected to the construction site tomorrow."

"The site will close soon, if you pull it off."

"How do you mean 'if'? Perdalonga is already itching to do it."

Marigosa sits on the broken wall that surrounds the second patio. The parcel enclosed in the paper roll crinkles pleasantly.

"He has lots of lawyers. Mossa-Sguincio pretends to be on your side because Tuvu gives him mushrooms and asparagus. But that's a person who takes but doesn't give. Perdalonga will make you sign a contract in which he undertakes to postpone the work for a few years and then ..."

"Then he'll die. And he's older than Sàtera."

Marigosa gives a full-throated laugh.

"Builders are eternal—like the land on which they build."

Gabola throws the razor into the lekythos and turns with his cheeks on fire. He looks even more like a kid.

"I must play."

Marigosa looks away, the desperation on losers' faces repels her. The fountain basin's full of earth, and the white scent of jasmine has replaced the water. Bees are buzzing in the orchard; below the grass stirs in waves, and the pine fronds make a sound that imitates the sea. The same sea, like the city, seems far away, fake, a theatrical set design. What a boring place! Why does Gabola hold onto it so tightly?

"If you knew fabrics, you'd know what happens to them when they sit in the warehouse."

"Tell me, what happens?" he grins.

"The fabric gets thinner, the texture gives way, yarn gets shiny. And then it's thrown out. It's impossible to cut and sew it. Consumed without ever having lived."

"Tuvu has always been used. Four millennia of use and it's still full of life. But Perdalonga wants to bury it."

"You'll lose this game." Then, resolute, she tears off the paper and shows him the full suit that she brought.

"You don't want to go to Perdalonga dressed like a peasant, do you?"

The excavator sinks its teeth into the earth and rips up clods of juicy grass, roaring with joy. A bulldozer flattens

the earth while raising dust, stones, and fragments of
cinerary urns. A pink cloud surrounds the machines and
workers. Here you're breathing the dead, together with
the smell of bent stalks. I'd like to plug up my eyes, ears,
and nose. And scream, scream with all the breath in my
body.

The worker who was waiting for me at the gate precedes
me quickly in the direction of a white box the size of a
room just below the sign, *Apartments for sale, penthouses,
offices, various sizes.*

Placing your index finger on the opaque surface of a
wall makes a door slide open, through which we enter.
The light of the sun, filtered through the walls, is cold like
well water. Inside are file cabinets, shelves weighed down
with figurines, urns, and fragments of amphorae. I catch
a glimpse of a mother goddess carved out of bone with a
nose like an owl's beak. They're digging deep, arriving at
Tuvu's oldest strata.

The workman gestures toward a desk, behind which
is a fat man in a jacket and tie who stares at me. His eyes
are yellow from liver problems, his skin greasy and pale.
I figured Perdalonga would look like that. Standing at
the side of the desk is the foreman, helmet on his head,
cement-colored mustache, and white shirtsleeves rolled
up over the elbows to show off the red-and-blue tattoos
that cover his muscular forearms.

I throw the net on the desk. The urchins crackle
and move their spines, splashes of salt water falling on
Perdalonga's iron gray suit. We're dressed alike. The knot
of his silk tie protrudes from the three chins that dangle
under his jaw. He sweats, I sweat. The collar of my shirt
pricks my neck. I should have worn my usual t-shirt.

I push the net toward him.

"Here's what you wanted."

The man sitting on the other side of the desk barely
raises an eyebrow. I thought I'd see the wild joy of greed in

his eyes. Instead, he calmly raises a bucketful of water from under the desk, looks for scissors in the penholder, takes an urchin, cuts off the underside, uncovers it, and rinses it off. The bucket water grows cloudy, the orange eggs shine.

He passes the clean urchin to the foreman, and Cement Mustache winks at me.

The man in the jacket and tie cleans the shells and lines them up along the edge of the desk, deferentially; his cuffs get dirty from the salty shit. Now I understand: he's an office grunt, a bureaucratic donkey. Cement Mustache is Perdalonga. The bureaucrat opens a refrigerated drawer and uncorks white wine, an expensive label. He offers me a glass, too.

The wine burns my tongue. I remember the taste of tears that I cried for Monzitta when the nanites drained out of my brain.

Look at what you have to do to win. It frightens you. I've never feared anything in my life, never. Not even the time when the ceiling of a tomb collapsed and I had to dig my way out with my bare hands. But now I'm afraid that Perdalonga will discover the deception.

"Where is the contract?" I ask.

Perdalonga drinks and eats with pleasure.

"Whom did you buy the skill from?" he asks between urchins.

"From Sàtera."

He emits a joyous hiccup.

The obedient ass opens a drawer and pulls out two decks of cards.

"Let's give it a try," Mustache says. "Cardia the surveyor is a great player."

He points to a chair while the surveyor shuffles and distributes the cards. The money is colored plastic chips, a "10" is stamped on the lower pieces. Ten erui to open.

I wear my best poker face, and I wait. The prickly fabric of my collar forces me to keep my head straight. That witch

Marigosa! She sewed a shirt on purpose that forces me to concentrate. Also, the shoulders of the jacket are slightly padded to make me look more substantial. On the double breast, instead of buttons, shine four Punic copper coins engraved with ears of wheat.

The game proceeds. In the fourth round I get good cards and try to lure Perdalonga into a trap. Money is always money. But he responds impassively to my raises. He has to have at least a straight or a flush. I withdraw. The surveyor holds his own for another two rounds and then surrenders. Perdalonga mockingly plays his hand: he only had three ladies of a kind.

Look at how things are going. Convinced that he's unbeatable, the builder keeps the bluff and manages to win with his own strength.

"The contract is with Mossa-Sguincio. Let's take two steps over to his office."

Outdoors, the air is warm like unrefrigerated beer. The bulldozers, the diggers, the pneumatic hammers, the steel monsters are always there. They roar every time they open their toothy mouths, but everything is different. The air, the sky, thistles, and clover are blackened silver. The stones are washed out as if they had been dipped in bleach, and I walk among the jewels of Tuvu with a heart like an ice cube.

An hour ago I left Monzitta and inhaled salt water and nanite mappers. I took the urchins that contained Sàtera's skill to Villa Mura and left it on the champion's gaming table along with a silver spoon I found among the stones. She was sleeping. On awakening she'll eat the urchins and be the poker queen again.

Perdalonga is chattering away.

"You're a strange type. You could ask me what you want, any figure. You would have become rich. You could even claim one or two apartments. I would have given them to you."

His safety boots crack the gravel as he advances with determined strides. I'm wearing plain imitation leather moccasins, black and uncomfortable. I slide with every step. Perdalonga lingers for a moment on the north side of Tuvu and stares at the expanse of buildings that cover Grand Tuvu, the neighboring hill.

"This city is comatose. You have to nudge it, give it a shake, otherwise it will keep sleeping. The dead are not just below." He taps the earth with his heel. "I meet them every day. The public administration is populated by zombies. Slow, slow, slow. But I travel at a different speed."

He starts up again, bypassing a jasmine bush. He takes one and brings it to his nose.

"My buildings are wonderful; I always look for the best architects. The Little Tuvu project is Kevser Mardin's. Walls and floors at a constant temperature, roof garden, bathrooms with steam showers ..."

I laugh out loud.

"Nobody builds exactly according to plan. The lawyer told me about it. Customers are shown a simulation that leaves them open-mouthed, then the variations are introduced. Eliminate the crawlspaces, resize the environments, scrape off a few inches from the ceiling. And the hanging garden shrinks, becoming two vases on the roof."

He puts his hands in his pockets and sways, following the serpentine path in the middle of the sea of grass.

"The architects are eccentric megalomaniacs. They get carried away. The houses must be simple and functional. And people need homes. You live on the top of Tuvu in that half-collapsed hovel, right? But you're young and healthy. I want to see you in twenty years—with osteoarthritis. Or when you have to trudge up the hill with two bags of groceries. Then you'll curse yourself and want elevators. When I was a boy here, there were people living in the tombs. Without water. Without light. I gave them a house. A real house."

"And you bought their land."

Perdalonga curls his lip, lifting his cement-colored mustache.

"But what are you, a savage? A wild environmentalist? Are you one of those people who'd like to go back to the Stone Age—without washing machines, without refrigerators, without electricity?"

"Then you started building the homes on the slopes of Tuvu. Six floors. The old buildings only had three."

"Times change. The city grows. Here there's a hunger, boy, a hunger for housing. I've always had the authorizations in order. My bricks respect the law."

"You make the law."

He shrugs and takes the path among the pines. A snail cuts across our path, and Perdalonga gives it the right-of-way, observing the damp silver thread it leaves behind. We resume walking. On the left you go up to my house, on the right you enter an area closed by a gate. Perdalonga draws a heavy bunch of keys from his pocket and throws open the door, gesturing for me to follow him. A little further, recessed in the middle of a hill, is a low, square building. The white stone clashes with the red earth like a sheet that's too clean.

"This is the reception center of Tuvu Park. All at my expense. And this is the park."

He points to a downhill path bordered by concrete that runs along a part of the tombs to the southwest. Stripped of vegetation, the openings look like many shaved and wide-open cunts. In the middle are transplanted rosemary and lavender bushes never grown on Little Tuvu.

"At the entrance I put two millennial olive trees. Do you have any idea how much it costs to uproot and transplant them?"

"You could have planted them many years ago. Now they'd be big."

"I can have them immediately, already grown. And

they'll make Little Tuvu an even more beautiful place. It's already wonderful now. Look at the velvety waterfall of grass. And the entrance to the pointed arch of the Catino. Even the abandoned blast furnace has its charm. Reminds me of a missile on a launch tower ready to leave for the stars. Here also the rust is beautiful."

The nanites hidden in the urchins are doing their job. Assaulting the fort of Perdalonga's brain, burning old ideas away, and replacing them with something else. Something completely different.

In front of the net that separates Tuvu from the office parking lot of Mossa-Sguincio, Cement Mustache bends over and remains that way, taken by something he sees on a bush. A white and foamy cocoon sways under a juniper branch. The caterpillar is emerging from its tomb. Maybe it's the same one I found wooing the rose water. The insect makes its way beyond the cotton wool, its little paw on top of the sarcophagus, and it opens its black, yellow, and deep blue wings.

"I've never seen anything so beautiful," Perdalonga whispers.

I'm sitting on the wall that slopes down to the lower part of the garden. Above me the pines rustle restlessly. Under me the wild parsley spreads haphazardly, nibbling at the edge of the sage. Here grandma had planted aromatics far from the sterile pines. The laurel has become a tree with corroded leaves.

I loosened my tie, took off my jacket, and rolled up my shirt sleeves. Next to me is the contract prepared by Mossa-Sguincio. Eighteen pages full of promises and commitments.

I pledge to keep intact the hill known by the name Little Tuvu. I'm obliged to dismantle the building site, eliminate fences and gates, rebuild the fallen walls with the same stones of the area. I take upon myself care of plotting the paths, which will allow entry to visitors, in material compatible with the colors and soil of the hill; the paths will respect the morphology of the terrain. I assume the responsibility of providing public fountains, trash cans, and benches for the contemplation of this paradise of beauty and serenity.

Signed, Giuseppe Perdalonga.

The wind picks up, lifting the pages, playing with them in mid-air and scattering them on the plants. There's something funny about this scene. I sense it, yet it escapes me. I look at the slope, the roofs of the buildings, the Lagoon, the distant mountains, and I feel nothing. No emotions—neither beautiful nor ugly. They are things. Elements of the world.

The house is a falling ruin, the sheets I'd hung out to dry its ghosts. I remove the clothespins and tear the fabric, which unravels in my hands.

Monzitta keeps running from room to room. He also rummaged in those without windows, inhabited only by pigeons and lizards. Sometimes he calls out: "He brought his grandma's urn!" or "The artifact copies are still here!"

Marigosa sits on the wall. The blue suit she'd given to Gabola for the meeting with Perdalonga is on a hanger near the washhouse, together with his old clothes. He must have brought a brand new suit to jump to the Italian peninsula. Marigosa feels a great sense of relief. And also a great despair.

Eventually, Monzitta leaves the house, muttering to himself. He grabs an overturned bucket on the grass and goes to the outside faucet. A couple of seconds after turning the lever, the wind rotates the blades of the windmill, the pump turns on, and water gushes out. Then he sits next to Marigosa, the basket placed in their midst giving off a powerful smell of salt water.

"Want an urchin?"

From the back pocket of his trousers, he takes out the

urchin pliers; with the speed of a gunslinger, he splits the animal in two and hands her the half valve. Without taking her eyes off the landscape, Marigosa sucks out the eggs and throws the empty shell down to fertilize the roses. After the fourth urchin a majestic serenity invades her. How bright is the color of Tuvu's grass. And the blue of the Lagoon rivals the sky's. The pines ooze a fragrant resin. The wind tickles the back of your head, but when it pauses, you can hear the beating of a butterfly's wing.

"I know that that demon played a joke," Monzitta says. "So I kept some of the urchins that he had to bring to Perdalonga."

Marigosa smiles and understands. Understands everything, Gabola, Little Tuvu, the jasmine, the bees, the tombs. With a cry of joy, she raises the half shell and throws it into the bushes. The sparrows fly away merrily, and Marigosa rises into the sky with them.

HOLES

I am the server.

I offer hospitality and information. I supervise everything. I have everything inside me, like an egg.

I open the door, I bow, I straighten up, I raise my right hand, I greet.

I've existed for three hundred seventeen years, five months, and nine days.

I welcome, inform, offer maps.

Door, bow, straighten, greet.

Administer, supervise, take note.

I can do all of these things simultaneously, and I still have room to think. I meditate. I like to meditate. I am an egg that meditates.

Open, bow, straighten ...

Sometimes I reflect upon the history of mankind from *Australopithecus africanus* to the first settlements on Mars. It takes me only 0.17 seconds. The time that I use to bow. Obviously meditation requires more time. 0.18 seconds, at least. I meditate on the evolution of the species. Evolution is a synonym of change.

Mutation, modification, alteration, correction, transfiguration.

Open, bow, straighten ...

The egg doesn't change. Unless it evolves into a chick, that evolves into a chicken, that evolves into ... soup. Like the primordial soup. In short, back to the beginning.

I meditate on my raised right hand, the palm open

like in the image of the aluminum plate on *Pioneer 10* sent into space. I wonder, though: will the extraterrestrials understand what that gesture means? Maybe it won't say anything to them, maybe they don't have arms, maybe they are smooth, closed, serene, like ... like an ... egg.

The egg has a beautiful shape, but as long as it's closed, it's nothing.

Or rather, it's everything ... but also nothing.

Door, bow, greet.

I meditate on omlettes. You can't make an omlette without breaking the eggs.

Break, shatter, crack, split, crush, reduce to pieces.

I open the door, bow, raise my arm.

Breach, collapse, contravene, transgress, violate.

De Sade, Inc., contacts me to offer their services: *What is full, with us, becomes empty. Do you want to tear off the mask?*

Am I a masked egg?

Do you wish to know what it means to be human?

Am I a masked egg?

We have what you need.

What is it? What is it? What is it?

Holes.

Cavities, gaps, openings, cracks, crannies.

I deposit a certain sum in the De Sade account to get ... holes.

They send me a reply with an attachment. They say to open the attachment when I find myself alone. I am always alone. There's no place for anyone else, here, inside the egg. I open the attachment. A very strong white light pierces my circuits. Pain. An unpleasant feeling caused by physical illness.

Torment, punishment, misery, anguish, agony. Agony agony agony.

Something happens to my smooth egg face. The skin softens, yields, melts, dripping downwards. I raise my hands, trying to hold it back, and my fingers touch the sticky edge of two wounds. Holes!

The pain subsides, has become a widespread burning sensation, and I ... see. I see! In front of me is a ghost. It is a pulsating blue oval. It expands and contracts, radiates its grace on me. Inside me. The light hurts me, yet I can't look away. After five minutes the ghost coalesces into continuous and defined lines. It is a lamp. A forgotten reading lamp lit on one of the workstations.

De Sade writes again: *What is tortuous with us becomes straight.* They offer me other holes.

I'm resentful toward them. I hadn't thought the holes would hurt. I don't reply.

A few months pass, and I watch. I watch everything. I can only observe. I am an egg with eyes.

I write again to de Sade and tell him that I want holes to hear with. They send me the usual message with the usual attachment.

I open it immediately. Ah! An acute whistle! The tips of two drills pierce my head from both sides. They are hard, hot, they crush me, pulverize me. I think I'm shouting. I only think so. The skin, diaphanous, thin, like the membrane that covers the yolk, it runs down my cheeks and cools, clumping in two brown-tipped plastic ridges.

"Hi!"

A child has just entered and greeted me, raising a hand. His voice bounces off the still warm and soft walls of my new holes, banging from side to side like a ball in a pinball machine. Every letter is a stone thrown on soft mud, imprinting its sign in the auditory canals. Auditory!

For the first time I hear the Badineri of Johann Sebastian Bach for flute and orchestra. It's not a row of notes on a staff. It's there ... outside of me, vibrating in the air. Ah! it's a sweet music, a warm cream that goes slowly slowly down into my new holes.

It's nice to have holes. I like having holes. Knowledge is the world falling into a hole. The human being has evolved because it has holes. Alice found Wonderland at the bottom of a hole.

I want more holes! Holes everywhere!

I transfer more money into de Sade's account. They send me a release in which I consent to all the holes that they'll perform on me: *What is new becomes consumed.* And then the attachments arrive.

This time the pain is piercing, ferocious. Incandescent awls hammer my body from the inside, hooks soaked in acid widen the nicks, tear the skin to shreds, small drills from the tip thin as a newborn hair slip into the smooth albumen of my egg and emerge from the other side after leaving me a hole of infinitesimal diameter. They're called pores, and they bloom like little spring flowers over every centimeter of my body.

The smell of camphor slowly begins to invade my internal memory, but it's not a concept, it's not a definition written in the five thousand dictonaries I possess, it is a real scent, intense, increasing in intensity, it fills me, it burns like salt water and then spurts out of my nostrils, dirtying the floor.

Holes. Holes everywhere.

The world starts to spin, colors, sounds, scents, everything is sucked into my new holes and inflames me with pain and life. It's unbearable. I have time to send a request for help to de Sade, and then I faint.

When I wake up, there are two company agents in front of me.

"I am ..."

I speak! The voice leaves me from a hole in my head and spreads through the air.

"Am I a human?"

"No, dear. You are a woman."

Secret Enemy

I'm alone. I have a lot of time. Too much time. That's why I dig down. To the bottom of myself. And I find myself alone. I have befriended my loneliness. At first I wouldn't resign myself to this plain, stripped-down room. I don't mind it anymore.

Six-forty in the morning, according to the alarm. I open my eyes to the room where I am a prisoner, a room that's spartan but comfortable. The shit-colored curtains are the first thing I see. Who would have thought to buy those curtains? Yuliano Nagai, the man with no artistic taste.

My jailor takes care of me. I push some buttons on the headboard, which open a door through which comes the breakfast tray, hot tea, and slices of crusty bread, butter, honey. A new day locked in here. I rub my eyes and press on them firmly; you can see beautiful blue flashes. I go to the bathroom. Yul is there on the other side of the glass, and he sticks out his ugly muzzle at me, pulling down his lower eyelids to show me the sclera. I nod reassuringly. He opens his mouth and shows his tongue, a repulsive purplish mat with rosy edges.

"You've eaten blueberries again," I reproach him. "You should be abstaining."

"Blueberries have Vitamin A and antioxidants."

"Your breath tells me that you drank alcohol yesterday."

"Two glasses of red. Just two."

"Do I have to tell you, Yul? Alcohol strains the liver."

He bows his head, contrite. His father died before sixty from cirrhosis, and he fears liver disease more than cancer.

"Blood pressure?" he asks me anxiously.

"130 over 90."

"That's high."

"Don't worry about it. Approach."

He stretches toward me.

"The color of your irises has changed, cholesterol is 196."

"Last month it was 190!"

"Nonsense. For a forty-two-year-old man it's fine. Give me your wrist."

He obeys and pushes his wrist against the glass. On the other side I imitate him and register his heartbeat. A little accelerated, but now I know Yul. Medical visits make him anxious.

"For breakfast, drink a potassium and magnesium smoothie and eat fifty grams of fresh papaya."

He rubs his hands together, satisfied.

"First, twenty minutes of rinsing with sesame oil."

He grimaces but acquiesces in rinsing his teeth without protest. These are the only moments in which I have power over him. I can ask him to do twenty pushups, to drink orange juice, to jump, or stay for a quarter of an hour in the lotus position. He obeys me but has a subtle method of revenge. When I return to my room, the breakfast tray has disappeared and in its place is a potassium and magnesium smoothie (i.e. banana and raw coconut) with a plate of sliced papaya.

I chew slowly. Every bite is a thought about the life that I lead: healthy, honest, and unhappy. After breakfast is shaving time, so I go back to the bathroom to watch him use the razor, a disturbing ancient object that forks like a compass. My presence calms him. Yul lives in terror of cutting his throat. Buy an electric razor, I suggested. No, the free blade gives him a silky feeling on his cheeks that he won't give up for anything in the world. Then he dabs scented gel on his face, and the smell of Vetiver Veritas reaches me.

It's a scent that speaks of wet and gray winters, of a man who is alone under a black umbrella of elusive glances, of close horizons, too close.

After the operation is complete I sit at the desk with a sigh. Sometimes I get the feeling that the walls can move, that they're approaching me one step at a time to narrow the room and make it ever smaller. Without realizing it I'll end up crushed by these walls.

The doorbell rings, and Yul goes to open the door. It's the Flower Corner's errand boy with the usual delivery. Every day an expert florist carefully chooses the colors and the best varieties to accompany them and lets us have four different floral compositions. It softens the house and shows off Yul's weath to his guests.

The jailer also provides for my soul, and from the same door through which breakfast arrives, I receive two vases. The bouquets are beautiful and nicely prepared but also mundane, with no real creativity. And yet every day I look impatiently for the arrival of the deliveryman.

Today there are branches of purple and red hibiscus, cream-colored roses, forget-me-nots, and white irises. Magnificent. In the bottom desk drawer I've set aside some pebbles that I made out of papier-mâché. Once dry, I paint them with the ink of a fountain pen, obtaining a realistic effect.

I've kept a hundred packets of refined sugar, leftovers from the period in which "Mr. Health Fanatic" was drinking coffee. An old upside-down chessboard serves as a base and container: I level the sugar and then rake it, inserting three well-sharpened pencils between my fingers. I drop two stones in a corner and take a few steps away. The optical effect is great: the sugar becomes tropical sand, the stones rocks.

I choose the smallest hibiscus flowers that I can find, and then I roll a piece of newspaper to create a tree branch, put it down, twist it, and get a white spruce branch, which takes on the color of the sand. With some elastic I attach the hibiscus twigs to the main branch and place the leaves so that they cover the bands. I keep the left side of the chessboard open and concentrate the color stain on the right.

Classic ikebana involves splitting space into three levels. The branch is the Sky, the flowers are the Man, the stones and sand the Earth. I walk away and scrutinize my creation. After finishing an ikebana I meditate on it. I work without reflecting, following my instincts, but then every composition tells me a story.

This makes me think of Yul. The red of the corollas is his passion, grounded by the sugar of profit, under the twisted sky of his sterile existence.

During the day I study the classical styles of texts that I've succeeded in procuring over the years. Shoka and nageire are my favorites. I recently found a book on avant-garde ikabana, which introduced the use of sheet metal, cardboard, wood, glass, and a greater compositional freedom in the arrangement of the flowers.

Night is the worst time. Yul goes to dinner with clients, stuffs his face with sushi and udon, then comes back to the house swollen and nervous. He stands in front of the mirror, raises his shirt, points his index finger at the right side of his stomach.

"My liver hurts," he says.

Nonsense. The liver is a silent organ. In fact, often when you discover a cirrhosis, it's too late to treat it.

"It's just indigestion," I reply.

"Should I get into the hedgehog pose?"

"Here, okay, do the position for a few minutes. You'll see that then you'll sleep like a baby."

He goes stumbling back to his room, leaving the door wide open. I can see him stretched out on the bed and curls up, bringing his knees to his chin and then rotating them left and right.

I go back to thinking about a new ikebana.

I would love to make a chabana for the tea ceremony, using only one flower and a few green leaves. The simplicity of the chabana is illusory, requiring, in reality, deep reflection.

One evening, while drying carnation stems on the radiator, I sense commotion in the next room. I look into my bathroom, and on the other side, in Yul's bathroom, I glimpse a stranger in a jacket pissing into the toilet, relaxing his shoulders with relief. He zips his fly and approaches the washbasin. He picks up all of the bottles, reads the labels, sniffs the fragrances, then washes his hands, and leaves. His place is taken by a young woman in a gray suit. She also pees and rummages through the aftershave, tonics, vitamins. She makes sure that the door is closed and then swallows two pills. Two other men follow each other to use the toilet. From the noise I guess that Yul's bedroom is pretty crowded. Suddenly the bathroom door opens, and Yul drags a large rubber air mattress over to the tub and presses it in.

"In the bathtub two people can sleep comfortably," he says, turning to a small group looking in over the threshold. "I'm so sorry, guys. After all, it's just for one night."

The guests are dissatisfied but resigned.

"I can't rest on a soft mattress," one woman objects. "I have a bad back."

"The couch is uncomfortable," echoes one man.

"Can we play Rock, Paper, Scissors?" mocks a voice at the back.

"Calm down. Now let's look for a solution," Yul replies, raising his hands. This isn't the first time he's brought home a head of cattle. He always deals with large quantities, a hundred and fifty, sometimes two hundred workers altogether, and when that happens, he can't find a place for everyone in the hotel, so some are then guests in his house. Generally, though, he arrives with two or three people; this time it's twenty employees, all equipped with side-arm briefcases, sober jackets, and a strong awareness of their rights.

Most of the herdsmen move workers from one nation to another and leave them to fend for themselves. Not Yuliano Nagai. He wants to provide us with a high quality product, a happy worker. I'm certain that for tomorrow he has already ordered a great catered breakfast and booked the taxi that will bring them to the workplace.

His beasts' welfare is an advantage for himself and for the companies that are looking for efficient workers at the best price on the market.

At night the bathroom is in turmoil once again. The woman I'd seen taking the pills presses her chest and breathes with difficulty. She walks back and forth in bare feet, in an ivory silk slip, while her bathtub companion snores with abandon, unaware and indifferent.

Not like Yul. He sleeps lightly, like any self-respecting cowboy. He asks her what's wrong, and the steer responds that she's worried about the next day.

"I've never worked outside the home," she sobs. "I'm used to my desk, my window, my cup of tea ..."

"What do you do?"

"I specialize in psychic well-being and workplace happiness. I should be able to calm anyone down. One time, during my internship, I managed to disarm a systems engineer. He wanted the company to use a more strightforward storage program, and to be convincing he pulled out a 35-caliber gun. I talked to him, and he handed me the weapon."

"I'm sure that in your work you're efficient and professional, but personal ghosts are another thing."

She covers her mouth and wipes her eyes. Those responsible for psychic well-being don't evoke the specters of negative feelings. Talking about it is like summoning it up, and the experts have been trained to sweep their emotional garbage under the rug.

Yul approaches the sink, chooses some bottles from the medicine collection and pours some drops into a clean glass.

"When I'm nervous, I make a mix of macerated linden, Rescue Remedy, and Neocalm."

He stretches out the cocktail with Lourdes water, stirs it, and offers it to the woman.

"My name is Kriszta," she says, introducing herself.

They sit; Yul on the toilet, she on the edge of the tub. Yul also drinks one of his relaxing blends. The night invites confidence. I keep spying on them until she yawns and resumes her place in the tub and he goes back to the bedroom. Then I return to my room with my heart in turmoil.

I like Kriszta. Young, but not too young, smiley but not silly. Yul is attracted to her because he can talk about psychic health and the opening of the chakra, but I would have wanted to ask her if her parents often left her alone. If she were shy and had to learn to pretend to be extroverted to live in touch with others.

Obviously I have no say in the matter. In all these years only Yul had romantic relationships. I've stayed on the other side of the glass. Relationships—do I need to say it?—that were disastrous. Sometimes I warned him: "She's not for you," I told him. Or, "She's cute but too superficial." Nothing. He was dazzled by a pretty face, only to hit the hard wall of reality.

Yul and I grew up together. Often, as kids, he'd stand on the other side of the glass and scrutinize me. Observing with critical eyes the development of my limbs, the growth of my hair, my muscles.

On those occasions I trembled. Yul was the witch and I the poor caged Hansel; he stopped short of questioningly sticking out a finger to see if I had put on flab. He cared about my brain growth. He wanted a medical specialist, any type of medicine—Western, Chinese tao, Indian ayurvedic, homeopathic. It was easy to take advantage of my isolation. I greedily read any text, and he selected books based on his own interests, certainly not on mine. Never once did he ask me if I would like a diversion like an historical novel, a simple murder mystery, a comic book. He read Bilal, soaking in the jacuzzi; I pulled my eyes out over pancreatic physiology.

Transhumance takes place the next morning. The herd chews croissants, drinks freshly ground coffee, then moves on to the workplace. Kriszta washes her face and puts her makeup on in front of the bathroom mirror. She makes sure that her colleague has already left and writes quickly with eye pencil above the glass. Her telephone number.

Rikka! I just want a beautiful, colorful, and festive rikka. The florist's errand runner delivers tiger lillies, peach branches, lilac aster, and grapevines. I get right down to work, also using the dry carnation stems. Yul improves. His cholesterol and blood pressure are down. He's stopped making himself a small glass of gin before going to bed. He hums while massaging the aftershave into his cheeks and winks at me as he confidently walks away.

My rikka is a blaze of pink and green. The soft wood of the vine, bent into an arc, forms the Sky, into which ascends a pink dawn of peach blossoms. On the Earth I alternated the carnation stems with the aster to remember what life was like before Kriszta. I put the vase in the center of the desk, and when I look at it, I feel my heart filling with joy.

"You can't stick your nose in my work!" she says.
"I'm the one who chooses the workers!" he counters.
"You choose poorly."
"I was responsible for human resources when you were still in college!"
"Yes, I know you're old."
Silence.

The bathroom door opens, and Yul staggers to the sink. He leans on the edge and slowly raises his eyes to me. He expects me to contradict Kriszta's words, but I only speak the truth. You're old in the head, idiot! She's right, the workers must also be selected based on their declared enthusiam. You were the only one who still relied on lie detectors. The best way to get to know someone's opinion is to ask them. And trust your intuition.

Yul fumbles among the medicine bottles, gulps down three drops of Mimulus, two of Tacalens. Through the bathroom door I can see the room and Kriszta going back and forth between the closet and an open suitcase on the bed, throwing in a heap of clothes, underwear, socks, and shoes.

Admit your mistake. Kriszta is teaching you something. It's time to learn, you jackass of a cattleman.

It's no use.

Yul is calm now. It's a pharmacological calm.

"Let me remind you that you work for me," he says, straightening up.

Kriszta looks out from the threshold of the room, tears off the badge with her name and photo hanging from the lapel of her jacket, and throws it on the bathroom floor.

The cattleman flinches, branded by the refusal of the working animal to submit to his orders. She closes the suitcase and leaves. Yul stares at me, a corner of his mouth trembles. He clings to the sink so as not to run after her. He reaches out a hand between the bottles and sprays a clear yellow liquid on the glass. In a fraction of a second, my senses analyze its composition: aldehydes, bergamot, rose, galbanum, moss, and ambergris. Kriszta forgot her perfume, Eau du Soleil. The droplets break Yul's face into a thousand prismatic fragments that roll slowly down the glass, bringing a piece of his soul with them.

The end of joy.

***

The following day at the usual time Yul is on the other side of the glass and shaves with his usual razor. I can't fathom what thoughts are hidden behind those empty, cold eyes. His vitals are all high, too high. The angle of the blade reflects my face and distracts me for an instant while Yul deliberately pushes the blade into his skin. A line of blood divides my image from his neck. If he decided to commit suicide, I would be dead.

"Heart rate 60. Hemoglobin 17. Pressure 80 over 102," I rattle off in a neutral voice.

He looks at me with surprise and staunches the wound with aloe.

"Today you could have a bit of a richer breakfast," I continue. "What do you think about sausages and aged pecorino?"

He nods happily. Sausages are one of his old passions from when he weighed twenty pounds more. I lied. I did it for a good reason. I'm here to take care of his health, and as Kriszta said, sometimes psychic wellness is more important than the physical kind. Perhaps that's why she could appreciate the colors of flowers and the power of scents. When she arrived, I heard, for the first time, that sound that breaks the spell of sadness and monotony, the sound of a laugh. But you managed to drive her away, foolish cowherd.

After the spicy sausage Doctor Nagai grabs the phone and looks for new cattle that specialize in the treatment of nervous herds. Kriszta made him discover how useful professional collaboration could be.

Yul made three appointments and then took a jog on the treadmill.

I sit in my room, looking at the carpet so as not to see the shit-colored curtains. It's twelve o'clock, but the deliveryman from the Flower Corner hasn't brought anything yet. Yul canceled the order. There will be no more flowers in this house, nothing to remind him of her presence.

My last creation, a jiybana inspired by cutting-edge ikebana, is withered. A corrugated cardboard sheet represents the Earth. The Sky is a profusion of white bells that hang from the heather branches. The chalices are dry. Man is depicted by an interweaving of serpentine branches, small red gerberas, and purple fresia. The gerbera are still alive, courageous, tenacious, but I don't want to water them anymore.

I listen distractedly to the voices that come from the other side of the wall. Yul is interviewing candidates. I lie on the bed with my shoes on and close my eyes, pressing my fists to my eyelids. The blue flashes don't appear. I would like to dry up little by little.

The following days are a photocopy of the first day without Kriszta.

Yuliano Nagai keeps going straight ahead, his life is like a rail car. Not a single unusual gesture or unexpected action. The performance continues as long as the sun is shining. When the light disappears, fear silently advances and jumps on him in the middle of the night. Then he wakes up sweaty with a racing heart and clings to his hawthorn and chamomile cocktails. When these lose effect, he tries other plant derivatives, juniper and wheat distillates, which he drinks in a Martini glass with an olive that floats on the edge.

These are the moments in which the real Yul emerges.

At three in the morning, I see him drag himself into the bathroom, distorted by fear. A human being's first and only fear: that feeling that spawns symphonies, sculpture, children, the conquest of mountains, and religious ecstasy.

Every end is a small death. The end of a job, the end of a relationship. Yul only likes beginnings. It must be for this that when he eats he leaves the last bite on his plate even if he's savoring his favorite dish. He doesn't read stories about murder because he knows that he won't get to the last pages, the moment in which the detective exposes the killer. He stops films five minutes from the end, remembering that he has something urgent to do, and switches off the holographic projector, and forgets that he has even started watching a film.

"You should've seen this coming," I tell him. "'Kriszta' contains the prefix 'cri.' 'Cri' as in 'crisis.' 'Cri' as in 'Christ.' Only that we ended up on the Cross."

"It's my fault," Yul mumbles with his alcohol breath.

"It's not you. It's her," I reply. How much does such a lie cost me. I get a sharp twinge in my stomach. I'd like to grab him by the hair and give him a good beating. Instead, I have to smooth down the frightened mouse's hair.

"She's a bitch. You can see it in her eyes."

I've got his attention.

"She was always pretending. She praised you, urged you on, did a thousand gimmicks, a thousand sighs, swayed against you like a boat on the sea, but it was all a show. Don't tell me you didn't notice."

Yul turns his eyes away to look for a life preserver, finds a glass next to the sink, and clings to it.

"You thought you'd met the one for you, but it was an illusion. Kriszta wanted to use you to make a career."

"Which career. I don't direct the companies for which I get the workers."

"You're really naive. You have fifteen years' experience in the field of human resources. You can evaluate the professional spirit of any worker from janitors to bank directors. You know the tricks of the trade, some of which you invented yourself. Kriszta the leech was here to suck out every skill and then gather a herd of her own to compete with you. The bosses would have blown you off. You would have ended up engaging only unmotivated and tired fifty-year-old workers."

Blinking several times, he moves his pupils with the greed of a philologist who can read a Sanskrit text for the first time. Kriszta's every gesture, every word, takes on a different light thanks to my interpretation.

"What happened was good."

"Yes, good," I confirm.

The next day Yul whistles while he chooses a tie and on the breakfast table are the remains of fried eggs with ham in butter. I preferred to consume fruit juice while sitting on the edge of the bed.

I am lucid and calm.

I've decided to kill him.

"Can I have more wine?"

"Certainly."

Yul refills Jacinta's glass.

"I'm glad you stopped that diet," she says. "Oh, there's nothing wrong with a bit of measuring, but you were becoming fanatical."

"I?"

"Yeah, the last time we met, you were drinking centrifuged celery leaves and eating salad without any dressing."

"And you said to me: *You know that some vitamins need fats to be assimilated*?"

"I'm glad that you have made peace with fat."

"Now I wear it without fear," Yul answers, caressing his paunch.

"You were skin and bones. Now you're better."

He rubs his forehead, unsure.

"The mirror also says so."

"So, I'm right."

"I have the impression that it's not working well."

Jacinta bursts out laughing.

"A dinner invitation with technical advice."

"I thought ... since you're here ..."

"You're the same lucky asshole."

Jacinta leaves her napkin on the table, gets up, and

looks for her bag under the coat that was thrown on the sofa. She takes out a device no bigger than a pack of cigarettes, white and smooth.

"Let's see the patient."

Yul leads the way to the bathroom and stops in the doorway as she advances fearlessly to the large rectangular mirror that's hanging over the sink. So as not to be reflected, Yul concentrates on Jacinta—small, plump, her hips delightfully wrapped in silky hemp, wavy black hair loose across her shoulders.

"Great, I see you keep it clear," she says. "The clearer the surface, the more information to read."

She unwinds the analyzer cable. Yul takes two steps forward, curious about where she'll connect it since the mirror is embedded in the wall and has no frame. Jacinta presses a corner down, and with a slight "click," a square portion of the glass comes off the wall and it opens.

One end of the cable disappears into that small drawer, and a cascading data stream illuminates the instrument screen.

"You made me worry for a moment there. On the other hand it's a prototype. It could have developed defects in use, but everything seems fine. What's the problem?"

"The weight is wrong. Yesterday I called on a neighbor and asked him to weigh me on his scale; I have seven kilos more than what the mirror says."

"Maybe the scale is badly calibrated. This is a very precise instrument, Yul. It scans your whole figure and uses an algorithm to give you your body weight."

Jacinta moves her finger across the analyzer screen, discards some information, and enlarges others to read them better. Yul moves to the coconut fiber mat.

"You yourself find me fatter."

Jacinta rolls her eyes.

"I said that you're fine, not that you've become a fat, formless man. Don't forget that the mirror watches over your overall health, judging your weight in relation to a series of data: LDL, HDL, uric acid, glycemia, hormones. It communicates complex data to you obtained from the analysis of many heuristics. You can't treat the mirror like a scale."

Yul slowly raises his eyes, and the man on the other side of the glass does the same. Both men are both tall and firmly planted with a heavy frame derived from his maternal Cuban genes. The linen yukata softens his figure, the smooth amber skin refines the image. The face features a broad forehead wider on the sides where he is losing hair; thin, delicate nose; narrow mouth; and dark, judging eyes.

"Sometimes I think ..." Yul begins, then stops, feeling stupid.

Jacinta encourages him with a nod.

"... get the feeling that he hates me."

"He who? The mirror?"

Yul squeezes his eyes shut and fixes the image in the mirror in his mind.

"Weigh me."

"Of course it will weigh you. That's it's job."

Yul looks down at the man in the mirror, so similar in his memory to the principal of the school he attended as a boy, but also to his mother, the solid Elpidia Cruz, descendant of healers and sorcerers, able to read his soul without raising her head from the text she was translating.

"You have strange ideas about the mirror's capabilities," says Jacinta, disconnecting the link and closing the secret compartment. The mirror resumes its appearance of an adamantine surface.

"It's just a machine. Use it and don't think about it too much. Or rather, reflect too much," adding a wink for the pun.

While she slips on her coat, Jacinta looks around.

"You don't do ikebana anymore?"

"I have no time."

"A pity. I liked it. Perhaps you should resume it. It relaxed you. Next time I'll bring a nice bouquet of special flowers. At de Sade we are developing Flowers for the Soul, the scent changes according to the mood of those smelling it."

"If I'm sad, they'll smell like bergamot and galbanum?"

"Quite the opposite. It will agree with your mood; if you're sad, incense and woods; if you're happy, neroli and petitgrain. It's a new psychological theory, feelings must be indulged."

Jacinta takes away with her the air of a party by the sea and warm skin.

The mechanical arms clear the table, a ballet of stacked dishes with a light touch and food residue drawn into the incinerator. Yul watches them work for some time. He has never disdained home automation innovations—he believes they are the natural evolution of human habitation. But the mirror is different. Totally different.

He returns to the bathroom and advances toward the reflective surface.

"Where did I go wrong? I'm willing to fix it but tell me where I went wrong."

The man, on the other hand, condescendingly arches an eyebrow.

Look at him.

A pathetic idiot.

For a quarter of an hour, I'm forced to watch his comings and goings while he waves his arms around, begs, asks for forgiveness, promises to change.

You don't fool me, Yuliano Nagai. You couldn't modify a fingernail of your selfish solitude. And I will be ruthless.

The following days are a whirlwind of work. He doesn't call up any of the candidates for the position of emotional crisis expert. Yul fears being outclassed by people who are younger and more prepared. Instead he enrolled in a course on managing work emotions and studies late into the night.

He gradually abandons his healthy diet and throws himself into fats and sugars. The fats sustain him, the sugar consoles him. He also goes back to eating meat: tripe with sauce, sweet and sour pork, fried chicken.

"Weight 180 pounds," I declare when I look at him. In reality my sensors indicate 95, but he can't know that. In a few months he regained the pounds lost from the vegetarian diet.

Now my mornings are noisy, rough. I cannot concentrate on my reading of *Modern Ikebana*. The bell rings early. To find work you have to be in a herd, and the future steers are anxious to be examined by Yul. They come in groups of ten at a time; they sit in the living room and chat happily among themselves. We must show that we're sociable, it's a must. And then who knows that being all gathered together in a corral is not already a selective test?

Sometimes I think that Yul has devised this method to get rid of me.

He knows how much I hate noise, empty words, high-pitched voices. And indeed I often have to plug my ears with two cushions and read the text of a book aloud. He doesn't suspect that his strategies only serve to increase my anger.

Work, herdsman. I will make you fall into the dust, you and your dull work. You'll kick for a few minutes, drool everywhere, then an opaque veil will descend on your eyes, and you'll be ready for the flies.

One morning while Yul was rinsing his teeth with sesame oil the data I was waiting for arrives. His glucose is 114, even if he hasn't had breakfast yet. His potassium is down to 2, the albumin has risen, together with uric acid, pancreatic amylase, and total proteins. The cholinesterase, on the other hand, is low. In these last weeks it foundered.

His liver has difficulty digesting all the fats and sugars that Yul swallows. He certainly doesn't clean it up by rubbing the oil with an authentic Indian silver tongue cleaner. He spits out the residue, washes his hands, and straightens up, waiting for the verdict.

"Weight, 271 pounds," I state. I increased the real number by 48 pounds to give him an unexpected blow.

Yul opens his eyes wide.

"But yesterday you said ..."

"I had a processing problem. Today I managed to correct it." He turns and turns again, repeatedly, as if he doesn't want to believe what he sees. I can alter the information, not the image I reflect. He puts himself in profile and smooths his fat down from his stomach to his crotch, pressing hard with each pass. Perhaps he thinks he has a planer instead of a hand.

A subdued blip from the bedroom. A message has arrived. He goes to check and leaves the door open. I hear him exclaim an "oh!" of surprise and mumble something to himself.

Kriszta wrote to him.

She'd like to see him. I miss you, she wrote.

Yul returns to the toilet, puts himself in the shower without even closing the door; the floor becomes a lake. He rubs himself well with the towel, perfumes himself, puts himself violently into his pants, which he is forced to fasten under his navel. He looks for his best shirt and tries to button it up, discovering that only his wrists have remained immune to the leavening. The fabric tears because of all the pulling. He tries other shirts, but the only garment he can wear with dignity is a showy colorful jacket he bought in Lagos. He replaces his pants with an old pair of Indonesian ones with soft folds and gazes at himself under my eyes.

The geometrical lines of the African shirt mask, in part, the roundness of his belly, and the oriental trousers hide the fat, but I send him the image of a lump of shit strewn with confetti. You'd have done better to just tear down the curtains and drape yourself in them, stupid muley bull.

Yul collapses. He falls on the bathroom floor and stays there with his wet ass and cheeks. He already knows that he will find some excuse not to meet Kriszta. It will take time. He needs time to lose weight. After sending her a message he gets on the exercise bike and launches into a two-hour Vuelta. At the beginning he's happy with the speed that he manages to reach, then realizes he's cheating and raises the slope ratio, the pedals become hard, every complete revolution costs more effort. Panting and snorting, he releases the handlebars from time to time to dry his face on his tunic, his calves hurt, his thighs are hard, his stomach grumbles.

He isn't thinking straight and throws himself on the first food he finds in the fridge, a pack of ravioli. He devours them raw, grinding the pasta hardened by the cold with the ferocity of a hungry dog. He's halfway through the pack when a heavy sense of guilt falls on him and crushes him.

Returning to the bathroom, he puts two fingers in his throat and vomits the eight hundred calories of pasta into the toilet.

Relief, distress, half an hour on the treadmill.

I sit in my room and flip through ikebana books. It's just a question of time.

One night I wake up with a dry mouth. I turn on the lamp next to the bed. What is this! A dagger of pain pierces my left arm. It radiates toward my neck; my throat tightens. Choking, I look for the bedside table to help me stand up and knock the lamp into the carpet. The lampshade breaks, and the naked bulb intermittently crackles with electricity.

I drag myself to the bathroom. Yul is there on the other side of the glass, rummaging among the medicine bottles in search of a remedy, some kind of lifeboat. It doesn't matter if it's homeopathic or allopathic. Right now he would drink his own piss if I told him it would save him.

Another twinge of pain—intense, deep. He presses the arm, breathing becomes irregular, the tip of a spear rummages in his chest, tickling the praecordia. He raises his eyes toward me, and his expression of silent fear transforms into a grin of satisfaction. He sweeps away the bottles, pills, and vegetable dyes from the top of the sink. The whole mountain range of synthetic health breaks, mixes together, crashes.

Yul stretches his neck toward me and finally sees me; on the other side of the glass is a man with hollow cheeks, always hungry, always unhappy.

For several seconds we remain motionless, looking at each other, dissimilar twins linked by thought, divided by pleasure.

"A signature here, Mr. Nagai."

The head deliveryman gives me the electronic register, and I sign on the screen with the stylus. Together with his men, he unloads and assembles wooden shelves painted with a splendid amaranth lacquer. The shop window, large and well-lit, is a unique white space with a cube of the same color in the center. Every three days I will display my creation.

The team starts to leave but flattens against a wall to let Jacinta come in. I meet her and shake her hand.

"Do you like it?" I ask her, alluding to the environment.

"Elegant and light."

"I'll put the compositions that are already complete on the shelves: the shoka, moribana, jiybana. And here on the tables I'll hold the courses. I haven't unpacked the material yet."

"Yul, you're very surprising."

"I've been thinking about it for a while. I couldn't just end things with the other job."

"The last time we met I found you looking so sad. You looked old."

"I was old."

Yul leads the way into the back of the store. Behind a screen that depicts the flight of a crane, I've set up a special corner. Four tatami, a low table, cups, and a kettle ready for tea. With a gesture I invite Jacinta to sit down. She takes off her shoes and takes a seat on a pillow.

I turn on the burner beneath the kettle, arrange the cups, the bamboo whisk, the tea tin. Among the other objects there is a small black vase with a long neck placed in a corner of the table.

"I had promised myself to think of a chabana suitable for the occasion, but the inspiration didn't come."

Jacinta rotates her head to look at the vase, thoughtfully. Her movement makes me notice a branch of honeysuckle threaded in the lateral comb that holds up her hair in a soft wave. She catches my eye and gives a hint of a smile.

"A prototype of *Flowers for the Soul*."

With an almost absentminded detachment I remove the twig from her hair and toss it in the vase.

A delicate odor of happiness fills the air.

Rebecca

Last night I dreamed I destroyed Manderley.

I was sitting at the dressing table, combing my hair and looking at myself in the mirror. Suddenly I realized that there was someone behind me. I smiled, thinking it was Max. He loved to comb my hair; he could make it glossy just working with a brush and his fingers. Those fingers were so delicate in my locks that they melted the knots as he massaged them between his thumb and index finger slowly, gently.

It wasn't Max. I glimpsed a skirt in the mirror.

"Is that you, Danny?"

Sometimes Danvers combed my hair. She wasn't as good as Max, her software didn't have a hairdressing program, but I had trained her to learn by observation.

Instead of turning around, I kept looking in the mirror. An invisible force kept me from moving my eyes away from its polished surface and allowed me to observe the unknown presence only through its reflection.

The intruder wore my red wool skirt and my cream-colored silk blouse, the one with the bows on the cuffs.

She came out of the dressing room, showing me her back, stomping her heels, headed straight to the door, her right arm stretched out to grab the handle. No! You can't leave! You mustn't leave!

I opened my mouth, but the sounds stuck in my throat. I could only watch the scene that took place behind me and my image in the mirror, paralyzed, my mouth open, terror in my eyes.

The scene repeated itself in the dream an infinite number of times: the woman coming out of the dressing room, walking toward the door, extending her arm, and at that moment I stiffen, try shouting to stop her, try raising myself up by fighting against the constraint that crushes my shoulders, forced to stay seated in front of the mirror.

Finally, my anger at being treated like part of the furniture overcomes my anguish; I can turn around, and in the moment in which the unknown person opens the door, crossing the threshold with a triumphal step, happy to leave Manderley behind, I open my eyes.

I'm in my bed, head on the fragrant, clean linen pillowcase, the blanket folded back on the side, the sheets crumpled by my hands during the dream. The shutters are closed, but sunlight filters through the interstices, accompanied by the loud cries of seagulls and the distant murmur of the undertow.

I'm still here. I'm always here.

"Ma'am?" Danvers whispers apprehensively from the wall intercom. Her flexible arms reach out to touch me delicately. "You were complaining in your sleep."

"No complaints, Danny. Draw me a bath."

I jump off the bed, and in bare feet I approach the door to the room. I stare at the polished brass handle. The dream woman opened it without difficulty and was leaving wearing my clothes. I force myself to put two fingers on the handle, then I hold it with my whole hand, the left, because, unlike the unknown woman, I'm left-handed. I slowly lower the handle, pulling the door toward me and meet the resistance of the bolt. My arm falls back to my side.

I return to reality.

In the bathroom the tub is almost full; Danvers controls the supply of water and the temperature directly from the kitchen. I throw a handful of salts into the water, the azalea petals come out, small drops of blood in the tarnished crystal of the tub.

"Is Dr. de Winter back?" I ask as I immerse myself.

"They came back last night." Danvers's voice comes out of the bathroom control panel.

"They?"

"Mr. de Winter was in the country with his new wife."

Danvers is silent, and the silence of her synthetic understanding is filled by my confused human ramblings. I knew that Max would have taken possession of the house sooner or later, but I hadn't forseen a new wife.

"What's she like?"

"Young. Awkward. A student of Dr. Wu."

I had met Jing-Mei Wu at a conference in Copenhagen, an excellent experimental physicist. I understand why Max took an interest in one of her students.

"And how does he look?"

"Tanned. Evasive. Nervous."

Undoubtedly nervous.

I lean forward, resting my chin on my knees.

"Scrub my back, Danny."

From a metal plate built into the wall comes a flexible metal arm that stretches and divides into a small hand with three fingers. It grabs the sponge and rubs it between my shoulder blades. I grab my toes under the water and think.

The second part of the Manderley project has begun: experimental verification. Max can no longer count on my help, so he decided to find it elsewhere. A young student of Dr. Wu ready to admire the great Dr. de Winter and prepare the experiment with diligence and care, which she learned from her teacher.

"Danny, do me a favor."

"Anything you want, ma'am."

"The new Mrs. de Winter must have access to my study. You're the housekeeper; show her the house and my PC system in the library on the table where I usually worked. Fill the room with azaleas and colored cushions; on the shelves, put all of my clocks, the funny ones, the unusual ones, the ones made of water, of gas, of perfumed oils. She must be a wunderkind; she must feel attracted to the library and feel so good she'll want to explore it every day."

"Should I also put the bronze cupid there?"

The bronze cupid! I bite my lower lip remembering that statue I bought with Max in Venice during our honeymoon. How much I'd wanted it! In an antiquarian shop with wings wide open, a foot poised on a small alabaster apple and one arm raised in the act of hurling his arrow. It had appeared to me to be the perfect portrait of our love. I hadn't thought that Max's arrow would be aimed elsewhere.

"No. Not the cupid."

I get out of the bath, and Danvers's remote extension gives me the bathrobe. I come back to my room and look for the cigarettes in the nightstand drawer; but a thin bit of smoke escapes from the ashtray; and on the edge is a twisted cigarette because, like a fool, I'd tried to crush it to extinguish it. I put it in my mouth and puff out my cheeks; the flame shines on the tip, and I still taste the delicate notes of Moon Spirit, my favorite tobacco. The numbers on the digital clock, projected from the domotic control plate, float in the air above the nightstand. It's 4:25 in the afternoon.

I approach a window, open the shade, and look outside. Beyond the scrupulously mown grass, you can see the sea, deep blue, the color of my eyes. It seems quiet, crashing on the gray sand in short strokes; but you just have to look up at the horizon to discover its true nature. It collects the submerged power, it swells, it is proud, it raises foamy crests up to the sun and captures the light.

A long time ago at a convention on particles a colleague wished to build a machine that bottles memories. As necessary, you could uncork a good moment like one pops open a bottle of Bolliger brut, Grande Année 2459. A superfluous invention, since the machine already exists: it's called memory, and it is part of the normal endowment of the human brain.

A cruel, inexorable machine. It turns on whenever it wants at a sound, a scent, a color. I remember the walks on the beach with Max; we'd arrive at the boathouse and then sit on the pier, listening to the sea. From the pocket of my raincoat, I'd pull out my tablet. He'd do the same, and we'd plunge into calculations, losing track of time.

When my head started buzzing with fatigue, I'd untie the boat from its mooring, unfurl the sails, and spin away from the wind, jumping on the waves like a dolphin and shouting, shouting with joy, with pleasure.

Poor Max. He suffered from seasickness. His body needed solid ground, immovable points, to function while I loved the precariousness of the waves.

I close the curtains with a firm jerk. I go to the desk to compress the cigarette in the ashtray, but I recover in time. I place it delicately on the edge. It won't produce even a gram of ash. Here nothing is consumed except my anxiety. Day after day, month after month. I sit and open my datebook filled with calculations and diagrams. I concentrate on the numbers, my faithful lovers. I found this old datebook in the bottom of a drawer; maybe it belonged to one of Max's ancestors who, luckily for me, didn't have many appointments to make.

There's a "seamstress 10 o'clock" and "hair dresser 12 o'clock" from time to time; the rest is all free. At the start of my imprisonment, I wrote all of the differential equations, but then I realized that I was consuming every white space, so now I hold several steps in my mind. It's tiring. I was used to entering data in the calculation program and letting it work on its own, but to be forced into strict concentration has the advantage of distracting me from all other thoughts.

When I'm tired, I throw the golden pen between the pages and massage my forehead. The results of my final equations are always the same: zero. The oracle of mathematics answers my question with silence, and I don't know how to interpret it, what meaning to attribute to it. Yet I must understand my life depends on these calculations, so I'm willing to spin the most elaborate theories from them.

I get back to work.

At lunchtime the metal panel next to the intercom is raised, revealing a rectangular cavity in which a tray of food is placed: curried shrimp, roast veal with wine sauce, asparagus, chocolate mousse. The same menu that was served downstairs. Danvers makes sure that the portions are plentiful, such that you can throw out a fair amount when the serving dishes reenter the kitchen.

Who knows if Max and the new Mrs. de Winter liked the sauce. Every morning, Danny gives me the menu sheet and leaves blank the space for the sauce, so that I can choose the one I prefer. In the girl's place I would have crossed out the menu and served mustard sandwiches and a mug of dark beer just to scandalize the cook.

I can imagine the scene: Max at the head of the table— he always liked to be in charge—working the roast knife to reduce it to such fragments as to make chewing a dignified and almost invisible affair; her seated at his right, breaking bread, playing with the salt shaker, talking about the radiation oscillator, the difficulty of finding the right metal for that experiment ... a good-natured cicada, a perfect chatterer who lightens Manderley's atmosphere. Because Manderley weighs on him, it's inevitable.

Or not. Maybe she's well put together: hair, thoughts, gestures. At the table, concentrating on the food like she concentrates on an integral. Her calm charms Max.

I no longer want the mousse.

I return to the window, open it a crack. I can open it a few inches, but it would be useless to shout. There's an electrostatic barrier in front of the house absorbing any sound, erasing my image. If a visitor were in the neighborhood, he would only see the walls, the windows, the roof of the house.

Sometimes a gardener passes by. At Manderley the gardeners are very discreet; they move on caterpillars and emit a very slight buzz. They have various arms onto which are grafted pruning shears, hoes, spades, and they're programmed to react only to the sight of weeds and disordered hedges.

I stretch on my tiptoes to enjoy a wider glimpse of the sea. The surf smooths the stones on the beach, patient, tenacious. The breeze smells salty, and azaleas are in bloom. I close my eyes, inhale deeply, and the wind brings me voices. They're coming from the lawn in front of the living room windows, but I can't see their exact position. A man and a woman exchange sentences in an irregular tone, now loud, now soft. It's them, Max and the other one. They must have brought blankets, cushions, and newspapers onto the lawn to lie down in the afternoon sun and laugh like children who've escaped from their nanny.

I hear other voices. I recognize the deep voice belonging to Crawley, Max's assistant, and the noisy sounds of Lacy, Giles, and Beatrice.

"... to publish ..." This word comes to me detached from the general tangle.

Maybe Beatrice asked Max if he wants to submit a brief report to *Time Machine* before announcing the results of the experiment. Or maybe she is asking the new wife what she's published. One thing is certain: the Laceys are here to ascertain Manderley's reality. This house is your highway to the Nobel, Max.

I struggle to close the window. Suddenly I feel weak, lost. I must have patience. I must wait.

The days follow one another in the datebook, and I circle them with a stroke of the pen, an antiquated ballpoint pen, until one morning it happens. I'm sitting at my dressing table brushing my hair when a stealthy catch on the other side of the door, smashes the monotony of my days. The key turns in the lock—three, four, five turns backward—and she's here.

I see her in a corner of the mirror; she stares at me from the threshold. I smile at her in the mirror; I manage to smile at her.

I turn as she moves forward, examines the walls, the bed, the desk, the curtains, the hour projected onto the nightstand—4:25, obviously—and the recognition ends with me.

"You're alive."

"I'm alive."

Max's new wife is awkward and doesn't know what to do. I point to a chair.

"Come, sit down. Can I help you?"

Danvers was right. She is very young. Dressed like a student at the Poincaré school, she wears little makeup and has an intelligent expression that gives me hope. She sits fiddling with a bunch of keys. He gave that to her, as he did with me when he brought me here for the first time, to make her feel like the mistress of Manderley.

"You've been bold. You've ignored his bans."

"Max is in London. He's coming back tomorrow."

"Be careful. He might have pretended to leave to test you. I'm sure that, since you've just come to Manderley, he's forbidden you to go to the rooms in the west wing."

She nods.

"He said it was an unstable area and that, for my safety, it would be better to keep me away from here."

"Of course. Max is so thoughtful. He even worried about letting you know that he's still married."

She straightens the folds of her skirt, pulling it down to her knees.

"Danvers told me that this was the room in which the famous Rebecca lived."

"Famous?"

She nervously touches her hair.

"Your application of the minimum spin time theorem. I studied it with Dr. Wu, and when I saw your calculations on the library screen ..."

A profound joy fills her, vivifies her, makes her straighten her back and lift her head.

"You were looking for a way to standardaize elementary interactions, right?"

She's more clever than I thought.

"Your first work was more brilliant than your later publications, that is, those written with Max."

She blushes.

"Where did you meet?"

"In Paris, at the last physics conference."

I give her an encouraging look, and she dutifully continues.

"Max was sitting all alone in a restaurant in front of the convention center. I couldn't find a place, saw an open seat at his table, and sat down across from him. He said, 'It's taken.' I responded, 'Yes, by me.' I introduced myself, and when I mentioned Dr. Wu, he was immediately kinder to me."

He was already setting you up.

From outside comes a thud that makes us both jump. A door slamming.

"Go now," I tell her. "Max could have programmed Frith to check up on you."

"Oh, that old mecha-butler?" she says, bored, but gets to her feet, disturbed like me.

I accompany her to the door.

"The next time that Max goes to London, send Frith to town to buy something that's hard to find."

She nods.

"Je reviens," I whisper to her.

"What?"

"Je reviens. The password to my computer."

Stepping over the threshold, I stay standing and looking at the closed door; on the other side the key turns in the lock, and the latch advances in the wall with every turn—one, two, three ...

If it had been an electronic lock, Danvers would free me in the blink of an eye. Max's advantage is that he owns an old house with mechanical locks. The keys belong to him. Only Max decides what can be opened and what must remain closed.

For several minutes I feel intense anxiety; I think that the girl won't come back, that she regrets having gone against Max's orders, or she'll tell him that she's seen me and demand that he make me disappear altogether.

But no, what am I thinking? Danvers wouldn't let him kill me.

I sit at the desk, try to calm down. She'll come back. She's a scientist, curious by nature and by trade. She can't not be like that. She'll come back.

Indeed, after a few days, she's back, anxious to tell me the news.

"Five space agency consultants are coming to assess Manderley."

"The Lacy presented the spectrographic analysis."

"How do you know?"

"I had prepared the list of experimental tests myself, and they had to be performed by internationally known scientists for the accuracy and reliability of their checks. What did they say the results are?"

"They say that, inside Manderley, fruit neither ripens nor rots, azaleas don't wither, the logs in the hearth consumed."

I clasp my hands together and close my eyes: it works. It works!

"I saw the calculations on your computer. You were working on a hypothesis of space travel."

Whispering cautiously, as if she were pronouncing irreverent words in a sacred place.

"I was here sitting at my dresser and brushing my hair before going to bed. Max, from the dressing room, was telling me that the space agency had assembled a group of scientists from around the world to solve the problem of intergalactic travel. It seems like a joke now that the Moon is inhabited and we can build powerful spaceships, but we haven't managed to find a solution to avoid the aging of the crews. And while he spoke and I brushed, I looked in the mirror, and I knew. I knew how to do it."

The girl rises to her feet, her face showing great fear.

"Manderley is your discovery."

"Visiting time is over. Short conversations, like in all prisons."

She doesn't move; I have to take her by the arm and guide her to the door. Finally she decides to take out the bunch of keys. Just before the door closes, I put a finger to my lips to enjoin silence.

In successive visits she's full of questions.

"What happened between you and Max? Why did he ... kick you off the experiment?"

"Cigarette?"

I open the dresser drawer, but she waves it away. I close it back up and take the usual one still aglow.

"You'll have heard that physicists after the age of thirty no longer discover anything significant. Max was already past that age when we married, and while still valued, he hadn't published anything striking. I was famous for that application of the minimum time theorem, which has remained a brilliant theoretical intuition and nothing more. Until now."

I wink, amused.

"Manderley was the ideal place to prove my hypothesis. Large, isolated, endowed with a lot of electronic equipment. The simulation of a spaceship with the advantage of being well-grounded on Earth. It was enough to put it in front of a mirror, the right mirror."

"The electromagnetic barrier."

"I spoke to Max about my hypothesis. I was thrilled to carry out such an experiment with him; we would have become more famous than the Curies. Max said we had to be cautious, not mention it to anyone, scientists are thieving and envious, like any other human being."

"Thieving and envious," she repeats.

"And then one morning sixteen months ago, I found the door to the room locked. Max told everyone that I had taken the boat out and never returned. The bay is crossed by dangerous currents, and the investigation concluded that I had sunk and that my body must have been trapped in the cabin."

The girl gets up and paces the room.

"Since we came to Manderley, Max barely sleeps. I hear him walking in the library back and forth. He forbade me to say your name. He doesn't want to hear about you. He erased any memory of you from Frith's primary storage; only Danvers remembers you."

"Danny takes care of my needs."

"It's all so unfair. Profoundly unfair."

I show her the lit cigarette.

"It's been burning for a year."

She stops in the middle of the room, trembling with indignation. I've done it. I'll be able to escape. Je reviens.

"Today Max returned to Manderley with some members of the space agency," she says.

"I could show up at lunch and tell them how things really happened," I suggest.

I turn around to put the cigarette down on the ashtray behind me, and in the dresser mirror, in a flash, I see her lift up the bronze cupid statue that she found in the drawer. A fierce pain in my head. I fall into the brushes and perfume bottles. I try to get up, but a second hit pitches me forward, my cheek against the mirror, which runs on the horizontal pins of the frame, and it leans down, supporting my face. Blood runs down my right temple. A guttural sound comes out of my mouth.

"I believed that Max had married me because he felt lonely in this large house," she says, while walking into the dressing room and sliding open the closet doors. I hear the ticking of moving hangers.

"I thought that he missed you. Every time he embraced me I thought he was comparing me to you, the great Rebecca, his only love. He trembled when he looked up at the west wing of the house, and I thought he was unhappy. Instead it was fear. Fear that you could escape from here and take Manderley away from him."

She leaves the dressing room, walking at a determined pace. With difficulty I lift an eyelid, and in the mirror I see her approach the door dressed like me—a red skirt, cream-colored blouse with bows on the cuffs.

Now everything is clear; the dream, my anxiety, the result of the equations. Zero. Soon I will be zero, Manderley will be zero. The commission will note that fire consumes the logs, the fruit rots, the azaleas wither because time inside of the house stays still only if a human being is alive and enclosed in this room; and soon there will be nothing alive.

With the last of my strength, I prop myself up on my hands and raise my face. I want to see the clock. The figures above the bedside table are still firm at 4:25. She puts her hand on the handle, opens the door, leaves.

4:26.

THE SUBSTANCE
OF IDEAS

I'm a fraud.

That said, you know half of what you need to know about me. I'll tell you the rest now, and it'll be the truth. I'm an honest fraud.

Damkina came up with the idea.

We'd known each other as kids, me and Damkina. We grew up in the same House. The Caretaker, old Samash, had reproached me in the past, saying, "Wherever she sets her feet, you follow, Nergal. You're not a person, you're a shadow."

In the kibbutz exclusive affection is frowned upon; everyone must be friends, collaborative, ready to extend a hand to the inhabitants of the other Houses, prone to ask for help without fear of unfamiliar faces, glimpsed at the canteen or during linen carding.

I prefer to handle things on my own and help only those who have nice faces; the others fall into my web of words and card, weave, wash the dishes, sow the vegetable garden in my place.

There was a place that attracted the kids of every House. Even if you had just started walking and were still stumbling, you wanted to go see the Ship. The young ones climbed along the steep slope, dangled from the flagpoles, collected magnetic splinters, and with those amused themselves by dragging other pebbles along; the older ones competed to hop on the plank—a branch stretched over the dark precipice that led to the Cargo Hold. But only Damkina entered the Hold. Among us Green House kids, she's always been the most audacious.

She made a rope ladder, stealing the waste from the hemp process, tied it to a large qur root, and then descended into darkness, conquering the interior of the Ship. I arrived soon after. No one else followed us; they were all afraid.

The Hold was vast, well-lit, covered with fine white sand caressed by a lake of clear water that, at noon, became turquoise.

The kibbutz, in the period between Famenoth and Mesore, suffers from a lack of water. The tarpaulins for nighttime condensation collection aren't enough; the wells dry up. I asked Samash: "Little Father, why don't we take the water from the Ship? There's a lot of water down there."

He'd answered me: "Son, that's accursed water. It's as salty as the goat meat on the feast of Tammuz. You need to avoid it."

And he gave me the stink eye, arthritic hands shaking, but I couldn't stay away from Damkina. She was my water, and Damkina couldn't stay away from the Ship for very long.

We spent entire afternoons diving into the liquid expanse, swimming from one end of the lake to the other.

Creatures of every kind lived in the water: red and black ribbons, calves that grazed the submerged prairies, golden-striped trays, pink chandeliers.

In some places the rocky bottom—velvety green and blue threads where silver needles chased each other—breaks into deep, dark crevices that, to follow them to the end, I'm sure, would have led to the center of the planet. One time we saw a greenish glow coming from the chasms and perceived the movement of an immeasurable body shifting a huge amount of water, and its waves bumped our immersed bodies, pushing us far like twigs in the wind; we swam toward the shore and sat in silence on the sand, hugging our knees as our teeth chattered. Not from the cold, I assure you.

We often lay on the beach to dry out under the sun. The subterranean coolness made it less intense. In those moments Damkina spoke.

"We come from the stars, and we happened by chance on Sargon. The Ship is the wreck of a spaceship; our ancestors were exploring this galaxy five thousand years ago when their spacecraft broke down. To fix it they approached this planet, but the ship fell out of stationary orbit and started to dive, increasing in speed minute by minute. Some, to save themselves, wanted to abandon their companions, unhook a part of the tail to resume altitude; others, instead, tried to avoid the worst and maneuvered it to land here in the desert. Those who attempted the rescue are the kibbutz's ancestors, the legislators of the community; those who thought only of themselves are the ancestors of the townspeople, the selfish inhabitants of Erech."

I knew these were lies. Or maybe not. How would you prove it? They were well-told lies.

The time spent there made us bold. Exploring the Hold, we had discovered that the main lake, through a series of side galleries, could be accessed by some secondary pools. Little light filtered through the slits in the rock above and transformed the pools into dark, mysterious bodies of water. Here we found the pincushions. They nestled inside of small rocky cavities under the water's surface. When I tried to extract one with my knife, it broke into pieces; that's how we discovered that inside, in the middle of disgusting grayish matter, there was a five-pointed star-shaped egg, soft and fragile, of a beautiful color like that of the Sun at dusk.

The kibbutz's inhabitants are always looking for new sources of food, so we tried to feed some of the animals of the Undersea to old Tza, Samash's pet sarg, who scarfed down anything that was edible. When we put the pincushion star in his bowl, he licked it with his thin tongue and devoured it at once; immediately afterwards he began to hop and roll onto his back, legs in the air, playing like a puppy. Finally, after being silent for twenty years, as Samash told me, he started to sing the pleasant, painful lullaby of the sargs.

"They sing only when their hearts overflow with joy," the Little Father explained to me.

They came from all the Houses to hear the sarg's song. Tza sang for three days straight.

"Old Tza truly seems like he's in paradise," I blurted out while I was lying down on the beach of the Hold together with Damkina.

"The reason is that the pincushions spend all their time thinking in there in their dark puddles," she began. "They think and think because they don't have any distractions; it's now millenia that they've been doing it. Therefore they've developed all sorts of concepts, deepened each kind of philosophical system, analyzed every mental category."

With the sand prodding my back, the Sun warming me, and Damkina speaking next to me, I would have liked to sing like Tza.

"The intense meditative work of the pincushions has turned into an amino acid," Damkina went on, moving her hands around in the air to sketch the atomic form that she was inventing. "The chain of amino acids has codified a protein, which is the main component of the stars, and thus the pincushions store the enormity of their thought in a comfortable and compact form."

While Damkina spoke, our tanned shoulders touched, and though I knew the depth of her navel, the shape of her breast, the curve of her hips, the hair that covered her sex like thin algae on a round rock, I felt more naked than I was. I jumped up and dove again. The cold water turned off my thoughts.

It seems sometimes that the wind brings the stories along with winged seeds that fly in the desert and sprout in the most unlikely places. In the heads of the wealthy citizens of Erech, they sprout the desire for pincushion eggs, and so new faces started circulating in the kibbutz.

The outsiders were convinced that eating the gelatinous stars would give them original thoughts; not extravagant ideas or dream visions but rather strokes of genius such that when one thinks the others are open-mouthed, applaud, and offer prizes of money, of attention, and say that they have advanced humanity by twenty years.

The townspeople considered themselves more advanced than us; they were rude, nervous, sizing up me and Damkina, acting like they were God's gift to Tammuz. But only we were able to get them what they wanted, in exchange for a nice bag full of money.

Usually we picked them up as they strolled unhappily near the Ship; they had gotten nothing from the other kibbutz inhabitants except bread, salt, and fruit—gifts due to guests. Damkina was very good at haggling, making the townspeople believe that the pincushions were rare, that getting to one was a heroic undertaking, and she never delivered an entire star, always half, or two arms, to confirm the difficulty of the task. The other half of the star was sold to the next dupe.

Dealing with the townspeople was amusing but also tiring; they had difficulty following a few simple instructions. One absentminded biologist insisted on seeing the place where the pincushions lived, promising us ten thousand laz. At first glance we figured it was harmless, so five thousand in advance and we lowered him into the Hold with the warning not to touch anything, not to take samples, not to insert fingers or objects into the crannies. Well, that idiot managed to get bitten by a ribbon when he dipped his stupid feet into the main lake. How the idiot screeched!

We brought him back limping and half-paralyzed to his helipod; he gulped down all sorts of antidotes from the vehicle's first aid kit, but his leg was turning blue. We reluctantly had to call Samash and Nin, the caretakers of the Green House, who were able to stop the infection.

The Little Father stared at me for a long time with his owl eyes without saying anything. We told him that the idiot from the city had been bitten by a scorpion. The biologist saved his skin, got his great spoonful of ideas, and gave us the rest of what we were owed. Ten thousand laz!

"Where do we hide the money?"

It wasn't a dumb question since, in the kibbutz, money means very little; mostly you barter what you have for what you need, the community provides basic subsistence, and no one feels the need to have what he doesn't use.

"We put it in a safe place," Damkina answers. "The nest of forks. When we get to a million laz, we leave here."

"Leave? Where?"

"To see the world. There are a lot of places to explore outside of the kibbutz."

"We don't need that."

"I want to see Erech, buy a helipod, and get to the slopes of the Tramonto Mountains."

"They're clouds, not mountains."

"The clouds are in your head, Nergal."

I looked at Damkina and wondered who she really was; after many years spent side by side, she had never spoken to me about such desires. She was resolute, almost trembling at the prospect of abandoning the kibbutz; I felt her confident anxiety about the future like the sharp smell of ar berries crushed in a mortar, and I became as small as a berry. After that there were no more stories on the beach.

Of course, we continued to fish the pincushions and sell them to the townspeople. She wanted me to accompany her to every client, but for some reason that has escaped me, the carefreeness had abandoned us both and despite much effort, we couldn't recover it.

I feared the inevitable disinterest that at a certain age turns you away from the brothers and sisters that have grown up with you in the same House. Marriages between people raised in the same house are very rare; maybe it depends on the fact that they've rubbed elbows for a long time, that when you reach a certain age, having pissed together is a cause for shame, not love.

Damkina started going around holding Sin's hand, that sucker from the Yellow House whose hair looked like a diarrheal camel had shit on his head. Then one evening around the fire I sat next to Tishtrya and kissed her. I knew that Tish was after me since she'd flirted with me when we were on duty together in the kitchen.

However, one time when a townsperson appeared in search of stars, Damkina and I came to an agreement again.

We soon noticed a strange phenomenon: once tasted, the pincushion stars became obsessions, tormenting the tasters and making them crave a second bite.

Many townspeople returned to the kibbutz with anguished eyes, mean-looking, more restless than before because they hadn't known what they were missing. Now they knew and wanted more. It was the right time to raise prices. I divided a single star into five thread-like parts, then each portion into fragments as small as a flaxseed. I finally enclosed this microscopic amount in a sagyz pod. Price: five thousand laz.

Unfortunately, all of this coming and going of the townspeople alarmed the Caretakers. They understood that something unusual was happening. Rumors circulated of illicit trade, underhanded activity. Damkina and I had educated and properly scared the townspeople: they had to shut up or their ration of pincushion eggs would be totally cut off. Some, though, were dissatisfied with the modest quantity that they could buy; they were fighting with each other. There was even a fight in the kibbutz canteen. Two townspeople were stabbed, and only the intervention of the Caretakers stopped them from killing each other. I was passing by that neighborhood by chance, and Samash gestured threateningly at me, as he used to do when I was a kid and he was promising me a spanking and punishment.

One day I saw Sin walking ten steps behind Damkina, an abandoned dog in search of caresses; that same day I had broken up with Tish and her vanilla scent, and I was so happy that I went straight to the Hold for a swim. Along the road I passed four approaching helicopters, a blacker and larger version than our helipods. They landed in the field between the Hills of Tammuz, discharging a multitude of black and chitinous humans armed with a flaming rostrum. They obeyed an unarmed man who gave his orders by blinking.

I felt uneasiness rising up from my toes to my fingertips and up to my tongue. I ran to the Hold and there found Damkina, who had just caught a load of pincushions. I counted twelve overflowing nets.

Those dangerous insect townspeople had come for the stars, and Damkina wanted to hand them over in exchange for more money than she'd ever asked before.

"It's not right," I stopped her, putting myself between her and the ladder. I was shaking because for the first time I was standing up to Damkina. "The townspeople have too many ideas, all ugly and dangerous."

She laughed.

"Do you think they'll be satisfied with your alms? Damkina, those are people used to taking what they want by force. Do you ever wonder what the people do when they return to the city? What ideas they've gotten? And if the stars inspire hateful thoughts, foul actions, even ... crimes, or the will to overpower other human beings?"

Damkina took a pincushion from a net, opened it with her knife, divided the star, and ate half under my terrified eyes. Now I understood what had changed, understood where the idea of leaving the kibbutz had come from, to see the city, to reach the mountains.

"You can eat it, too, Nergal, taste it," she said, putting the other half of the star in the palm of her hand.

"No!" I backed away disdainfully.

She picked up the nets, lashed them together with a rope, and headed toward the ladder, turning then to look at me as one looks at a beautiful and distant place where one was happy a long time ago.

My heart in turmoil, I presented myself to Samash.

"Little Father, I have a confession to make."

"Better late than never," he muttered. "Speak, guilty shadow."

The Caretakers summoned the kibbutz's inhabitants and explained that our quiet life was threatened by the presence of evil people. Together we opened the Tammuz Gorge, and we hid in the underground shelters. Throughout the night Tammuz's breath passed over the Gorge, and the day after, everything in the kibbutz and around it was covered in kefer, very fine sand. Our farming machinery had been protected, but the strangers' hovercraft and the gears of their weapons were saturated with tiny white particles; every mechanism was clogged. The townspeople were forced to return to the city on foot.

I turned to the Ship and discovered that the sand had almost completely filled it, the Hold, the beach; the lake didn't exist anymore. I went to the Green House with a sinking feeling. Nin, the Little Mother, told me that Damkina had been there, taken some food, and left. I looked for the nest egg in the nest of forks, five hundred thousand laz were there, exactly half of what we had accumulated. My half.

So now you know the truth, the pure truth, because I can't make up stories. I can cheat the people. I'm so good at deceiving that I scammed myself. I thought I was fishing and selling pincushion eggs for money; instead, I did it for her. Only for her.

Now I lie down on the white sand on top of the Ship

and feel cold. The sharp granules irritate my skin. I tried to dig, and I found gray, greasy, dull water. Sometimes Tishtrya comes to see me. At night we join in silence; during the day we don't even glance at each other. But Samash looks at me worriedly.

One morning he calls me into the icebox with the excuse of helping to repair the insulation. He uncovers a pot full of frozen barley and pulls out a small metal tin. Inside, still well-preserved, is a whole pincushion.

"I bought it from one of the first strangers to try to understand what you were planning," he explains to me.

My eyes fill with tears.

What can the eggs reveal to me that I don't already know? I should have thought first, understood first, tasted them with her.

The tears fall on the pincushion, and its black spikes move. It's still alive. The salt water from my eyes has woken it up.

CREATIVE SURGERY

Early last summer, tired of focusing my attention on interesting pursuits, I decided to throw myself into something of no importance at all.

That was how I met Vi.

Vi had placed an ad on the notice board of the Institute of Creative Surgery. *Seeking welder for macroorganisms. Only top performers need apply. Payment in onions and fresh produce. Stern Labs.*

Unlike most students and even some professors, I appreciated the taste of fresh onions and of natural produce, and the idea of spending all day sticking mice paws onto bird bodies appealed to me. I love simple and repetitive work, the kind that doesn't require you to think.

I found the building, and I knocked on the door under the nameplate *V.T. Stern.*

No reply.

I knocked again and strained my ears to check if I could hear any noise from the other side of the door. It seemed that the lab was empty. I knocked again but to no avail.

I was just about to leave when I was stopped in my tracks by a concerto of rattling and scrapings of chains and locks. Then the door opened a crack.

"Who are you? And what do you want?" said a brusque voice.

"I read the ad, and ..."

"Come in. And no gossiping."

Vi was a nerd. She had all the trappings of a nerd: cropped hair, wrinkles from insomnia, pale almost transparent skin, eyelids at half mast and dark bags under her eyes. Good God, those bags! They were like two cobalt-colored beaches on which the turquoise waves of her irises broke.

She wasn't ashamed of them. In fact, she wore them the way other women wear earrings. They formed part of her face on par with her rounded chin and thin lips. Not many people go out nowadays with their own face; nowadays everyone is all sugary, fleshed out, and smoothed off; everyone's face is a blackboard waiting for the duster.

Vi's skin was too tight around the cheekbones and too slack around the mouth. It was covered with little moles, keratoses, and chromatic imperfections. She had silky hair above her upper lip, and one nostril was larger than the other one.

Apart from that, she was like anyone else without any features worthy of note. Her body indicated that she was of the female sex, but I had never considered that to be a defect.

She smelled like someone who had no time for deodorants or shampoos.

"Did you bring it?" she asked me.

"Bring what?"

"Your soldering iron."

I stretched out my arms and twirled around.

From her expression I could see that there had been a misunderstanding. She squeezed her eyes into slits and assumed the position of a serpent about to strike. But before she could kick me out, I grabbed a swallow's wing from a shelf, and with just the right pressure of my fingertips, I welded it onto the back of a spider that was sitting in its web in the corner.

The wing, animated by the energy of the spider, started

flapping, and it fluttered around the room. The spider waved its legs around frantically as the wing flew upwards in a spiral, unguided by any instinct of flight.

Vi grabbed my hands, turned them over, and examined my fingertips.

"Subcutaneous microprocessors," I explained. "I am a very refined welder."

"I don't want any gossiping," she said, pointing a finger at me.

I literally sealed my lips by brushing the tip of my right forefinger over them. She looked at me spellbound, and I felt like a stage magician. With my left forefinger I unsealed my lips again.

"We will get along all right, you and I," she said. "I'll show you what I'm working on."

Unlike her person, the lab was squeaky clean and full of the usual body parts seen in all the butchers' shops in the department. Two right arms, a left foot, three pinkies (one missing the nail), a collection of ears ranging from the hairiest (an auricle boasting curly blond fuzz reminded me of my last girlfriend's pubic hair; and for a second I wondered what it would be like to fuck an auditory canal) to the smoothest, pale-fleshed ones.

A row of meaty buttons like raviolis on a floury plate piqued my curiosity. Navels! All belly buttons like little domes, hairless and tender. I had the urge to pass the palm of my hand over them to see if they would contract, like turgid nipples. And what a show of colors! From mother-of-pearl blue to dragonfly wing green, and all the shades of red down to deep Burgundy.

"I see that you passed Anatomy," I commented.

"My best mark."

The higher your mark, the more body parts you are given.

"What is your goal?"

"To make money."

***

It was called "creative surgery," and at that time it was at the forefront of technical progress.

Apparently very simple, it was all about joining limbs, crania, bodies, eyes, and ears of different origins to create unusual animals, but in reality it was a sophisticated art. Most practitioners just produced badly assembled and clumsy chimeras—crocodile legs stuck onto a seal's body, a hyena's head sewn onto the body of a penguin. Expert surgeons, who could carry out an angioplasty with their eyes closed, debased themselves and became like sadistic, bungling schoolboys attempting to fix their torn teddy bears. My aunt owned a Devon Rex cat with webbed feet so that, apart from not shedding hair, it didn't scratch her furniture—a ridiculous creature that meowed and wiggled its ass like a duck.

With Vi it was a different story. She really was creative.

Our first project was a torto-cat.

She procured an impure Siamese on the black market at the Basic Genetics faculty: elegant head, turquoise eyes, short bluish gray fur. After the anesthesia, she cut off its head and legs, an unusual and irregular excision. Then it was my turn: I welded the cat's limbs onto a tortoise shell, from which shreds of rough skin still hung. I had to undo and redo the welds several times while she helped me by separating the flaps of skin from the irregular incisions with the forceps. She explained to me how to proceed, calmly, one point at a time, working with her fingers now on one side of the cut, now on the other side, so that the silver grey fur of the cat would blend in naturally with the epidermis of the tortoise.

In fact, both of the input animals had in turn been created and selected on the basis of certain characteristics: the cat had the smallest cranium that Vi was able to find to make it easier for it to retract its head into the shell.

Even its ears were small as Vi had had the foresight to use Chihuahua's ears, onto which she had grafted feline fur.

She was a perfectionist. She wanted every component of the chimera to appear natural, and the most difficult part of the work was still to begin. By using stem cells from some of the cat's internal organs, we were able to make them grow back again inside the shell. The cat's heart, liver, intestines, and stomach grew again inside the small space like the sails of a ship in a bottle.

Then we revived the creature.

This was the critical moment. Sometimes, in spite of all the precautions taken, undesired features of the secondary animal would manifest themselves in the primary animal. We ran the risk of having a cat that was as silent as a tortoise or that moved too slowly.

The cat opened its eyes, stretched its limbs, and meowed weakly. At least its voice was correct. Over the next few days we fed it intravenously and then it moved on to a liquid diet. Vi entrusted these menial tasks to me, and she devoted herself to some other work—a lapdog covered in a velvety fuzz that formed a delicate lace over its body.

When the cat was able to move about on its feet, making the green- and brown-plated tortoise shell sway, we discovered that the animal had a little defect, after all: it refused to eat the bits of fish I gave it but stole lettuce from the garden instead.

In the lab there was a large, sliding French door that looked onto a patch of tilled earth enclosed by two walls that met at an angle. Five parallel furrows housed onions, squash, runner beans, and other vegetables. Vi only ate what she grew herself.

I caught the torto-cat devouring the corn salad and shut it up in a cage.

"It's vegetarian!" I announced.

Vi shrugged her shoulders.

"It's the ideal cat for dog owners."

"Dogs?"

"Yes, when they try to bite it, they'll get a surprise."

Vi's eyes were shining bright. Now I understood the iron filings in the food of the original tortoise.

Our first chimera soon found an owner: old Pavlova, famous for her breeding of pedigree dogs.

She turned up escorted by three large Newfoundlands, white and shiny like new fallen snow and scary. Even though the lady was a champion of racially pure pedigrees, her bodyguards had Labrador heads, the glaucous eyes of Huskies, and shark's teeth. Even Pavlova herself, from under the veil of her hat, had the bright-eyed look of a killer predator; but as soon as she saw the torto-cat, her expression softened so much that she seemed like a sweet, little old lady wearing Mitzouko perfume.

"I've always wanted a cat," she said, stroking the clever creature's soft, little head. They were both purring with pleasure. "Ever since I was little. But I never could, on account of the dogs. They would have torn it apart."

She asked about how to feed it and look after it. Then she pulled out a wad of cash. Cash only, please!

Vi was not at all interested in the monetary aspect of the work and left all that to me. She shouldn't have done so because, with a part of the money, I immediately bought a dozen injections from the students hanging out in the hall of the Molecular Biology Institute.

"Kieser," Aye, my dealer, greeted me. "So, you're alive".

"And I intend to remain so," I replied. "I'm not a Black Vitalist like you stinking biologists".

He gave me a stupid look like a sad fish.

"Biology is destiny."

I would have spat on the ground in contempt if we hadn't been in his territory. A hoard of emaciated biologists were swarming all around us, waiting for a tidbit of organic material to study or to replicate. Every time I entered that building I wrapped a foulard tightly around my head so as not to lose even a hair. I wouldn't like to see my features in some experimental homunculus or come across a grasshopper that spoke with my voice. Long, thin fingers were groping at my legs while someone was feeling my cock through the folds of my trousers and someone else was trying to scratch epithelial cells from my sandaled feet; but I had sprayed a layer of transparent film all over my body and could suppress my erection using Tao mental control techniques.

"Show me the gear," I said, waving a fistful of crisp, clean banknotes under Aye's nose.

"I like your style."

He gave me a little rosewood box. Inside, lined up on dark velvet, there were ten needle-operated micro-inoculators.

"Pituitary?"

"Of the best quality!"

I looked for a quiet spot under the willows in the university garden, and I shot them all one after the other into my scalp. I had to wait until my eyes stopped watering, then I took out my hand mirror and examined my face carefully. It would take at least ten days before the effects of the hormones would become visible. In the meantime I noted that the interruption in my treatments had not done me any good: I had the same face as a year ago.

When I got back, Vi was there drinking a glass of vegetable juice and participating in an online meeting via satellite. Her usually neat and tidy laboratory looked rather overcrowded. Hundreds of men and women, young and old, were sitting cross-legged on the floor like frogs in a pond, their eyeballs trained on a large, bipedal toad who was haranguing them with a persuasive voice.

"You must want her! You must invoke her! I tell you that no one can know Grace if you don't have Fortune."

It paused and checked the reactions of the audience: open-mouthed gullibility.

"Can you feel the vortices of Fortune swirling around you? Can you feel the winds of Fortune caressing your skin?" continued the preacher. "You must seize her! Hold her in your hands and don't let her go. Fortune has wings, and she will try to escape; but the harder she struggles, the harder you must hang on tight, as Jacob did with the Angel. You must make her bless you! Only Fortune can give you what you most desire: riches, health, honor, beauty. You must yearn for her! Fortune cleaves unto he who desires her most passionately. Can you desire with such intensity?"

"Yes!" replied the crowd from all over the world.

"Yes!" retransmitted the satellite.

"Yes!" also shouted Vi, lifting up her arms.

"Call her!" ordered the preacher. "Courage! Call her! Fortune! Fortune! Fortune!"

At each word he punched his fist into the palm of his other hand.

His followers, young and old, males and females, imitated his gesture, and the laboratory rang with their voices, which intoned: Fortune! Fortune! Fortune!

I sat down next to Vi, walking through the crowd of assertive ghosts, and she looked at me: in an instant the crowd disappeared. I had made her lose her concentration and thus contact with the satellite. The preacher also popped out of existence like a soap bubble, and silence returned.

"I'd never have believed it," I said.

She took off her monocle, which was linked to an earphone.

"If you had been born naked, you would also trust in Fortune."

"We were all born naked."

She shook her head.

"My father is able to transform anything he touches. Bits of wood, rope, boxes, rings, every object obeys him and becomes something else, a flying sled, a puppet theater, a dolls house ... and my mother can materialize anything she thinks of just by expressing it out loud."

"She must have to be very careful of what she says then!" I joked. But I was impressed. Vi's parents were two very powerful Barums.

"Yes, she speaks little and measures every word."

She remained silent for a few seconds, immersed in a private misery.

"I was astonished when she would say *chocolate pudding on the table* and a perfect creamy, sweet pudding would appear," she went on. "I used to play with the animated toys my father created for me, but no matter how hard I tried, I wasn't able to lift a chair with my mind when my ball rolled under it. I could repeat the words *walnut ice cream* forever, but nothing would ever appear. The children of Barums usually show their talents immediately. At first my parents would say *maybe she's a latent; maybe she'll manifest later*. But instead, when I was five, to get dressed I still had to open the wardrobe with my hands. And to reach the shelf where my dolls were kept, I had to climb onto a chair. When I was sixteen I understood that I was naked. A normal, everyday girl who would have to study chemistry, physics, and biology if she ever wanted to alter matter."

A cabbage butterfly passed between us with a fluttering of mechanical wings. It struggled to flap its two enormous, dark green wings that were too big for its slender three-section body. Each beat was accompanied by a rhythmic grinding. Vi swatted it with her hand, and little wheels scattered all over the floor.

"You created the torto-cat. It's not a genetic hodgepodge or a badly assembled puppet. It's a real chimera," I said.

She gave me an ambiguous look over her purple eye circles, and her subtle mouth twisted into a grimace. "You haven't been going around gossiping about what we do here, have you?" she asked.

As an answer I welded my lips shut with my finger. She brushed the subtle line of the weld with her fingertips.

Was she checking that they were really welded shut? Was she attracted to welds? I only know that my throat tightened and my heart skipped a beat. Then she got up and went to work in the vegetable garden, leaving me sitting on the floor like an idiot with the beginnings of an erection between the folds of my trousers.

The torto-cat was our Trojan horse. Vi had managed to soften old Pavlova's heart, and from then on, she would send us her "leftovers," i.e. puppies whose fur was not quite shiny enough or not the right shade of color, those that had nonstandard ears or a twisted tail.

If students had a hard time finding organic material on which to work, imagine how hard it could be for them to find live, healthy animals. But for us it was different. Every Saturday Pavlova would select the newborn puppies, and every Monday a courier would knock on the door, and shout, "Parcel!"

I would sign the receipt and take possession of a box that stank of vomit and wet hair to the sound of whining and yelping. I would open the box, and twenty bright eyes would look up at me in the hope of receiving warmth and food. Like all our puppies, they didn't know that their fate was to be transformed.

The state of the art in biology only contemplated two forms of mutation, and Vi refused to follow either one.

"Neither cancer nor genes," she had explained to me. "This is a factory. Actually, it's a tailor's shop."

It was, in fact, more like a workshop: she designed the models, chose the living materials, and still yelping, she assessed the decorations, eyes, teeth, paws, tails, and then she cut in her oblique and irregular style. Then it was my turn, a human stapler. I put everything back together as per her detailed instructions.

She had an unusual goal: ugliness.

"Repulsiveness is the new attraction," she explained to me while she was planning to join the body of a miniature Pinscher to the great head of Rottweiler.

"Maybe you're right. The only problem is supporting a cranium that weighs three kilos on a body that barely weighs half as much."

From the instrument trolley she took a metal ring, and with the brusque gesture of snapping open a fan, it telescoped in a series of concentric circles all joined together: a steel neck.

"I've never welded living flesh to metal before."

"Well, now's the time to see if you can."

She was always so sure of what she wanted. When I was with her I was able to believe that I could do anything, that all I needed was to take just one more step, make just one more little effort, et voilà, the most elusive thing was within my reach.

She waited, patient and focused, for me to decide to act while she held a strip of muscle with a pair of tweezers just above the first ring. I stretched out the pinkie of my right hand—I always used that finger for tricky connections—and I pressed down delicately.

"Like that. Keep it there. Don't move. Wait."

Her voice, muffled by the mask, was a hoarse and passionate whisper. The metal was heating up slowly. The dark red fibers stretched and softened while the fluids hissed with the lightness of champagne bubbles. Drops of sweat trickled into my eyes, and I had to bat my eyelids to get rid of them. This meant that the hormones were working and had made me lose the thick arc of hair that had recently crowned my orbital bone.

"Now! Let go!"

I removed my finger. It was pulsating, red and inflamed, but the joint was perfect, invisible. It really looked like the muscles and tendons of the Rottweiler's head grew out of the steel ring.

I was amazed by the nature of the result.

After five days' convalescence the dog was on its feet, and the laboratory echoed with the sound of barking. Vi had been able to conserve the Rottweiler's powerful throat. In the absence of the mighty chest, the animal used its new neck as a sounding board. The result sounded like the Hound of the Baskervilles howling inside a boiler tube, distant and unsettling enough to make your skin creep.

The animal walked erect and proud on its miniature Pinscher paws, making a delicate pitter patter sound while the ruff of the metal circlets gave it an air of an Ottoman Janissary when it was stretched out and a certain likeness to Queen Elizabeth I when retracted.

I wasn't sure what we were supposed to do with the regal mutt, but my task was to feed it. That meant that I had to prowl around the department, scavenging in the bins of the operating theaters. It wasn't fun. I had to fight over bones with students studying for their anatomy exams. You can imagine how aggressive they became as their examination dates loomed.

On the other hand, for hearts, lungs, bits of liver, and intestines, I had to fight researchers from microbiology and pharmacology, who needed tissue on which to carry out their experiments.

At lunchtime, when the operations finished, I would wait outside the door of an operating theater with my metal container, surrounded by a surging mass of crazed students who shoved me and tried to climb over me. I received elbows, fists, slaps, spits, and bites. Thankfully, the pituitary hormones had inflated my pectorals, biceps, and deltoids. My back could have withstood a battering ram. I was a bastion of muscles like a dam against a tide of monsters!

A nurse would stretch out buckets to us on long poles, and we would descend on the bloody contents, strewing the entrails all over the place. Intestines were won by whomever pulled the hardest; bits of heart would slip from hand to hand like a freshly caught fish in a second-rate comedy sketch. They were won by whomever had the courage to take hold of one in his teeth and scamper away like a bear with a trout in his mouth.

I had participated in the past in fights like this in order to win a seat in a lecture hall, to listen to the lecturer live. The lecturers all spoke very softly, and only those sitting in the first rows could hear anything. Rich students would buy video recordings of the lectures while the poor ones fought for seats.

Back at the lab, I would boil up the bits of meat then I would purify and distill the proteins to nourish the pup by transfusing them directly via a feeding tube. After a while its hair recovered its shine, and its nose stopped being dry. Vi then ordered me to take it for a walk around the university.

"A proper walk like a real gentleman—no rushing, no fear. Do you know how to strut?"

"Sure!"

I lifted up my arm, flexed the muscles, and showed her my new body in all its masculine power.

First she was surprised, but then she frowned, and asked, "What are you taking?"

"Good stuff," I replied, "judging by your reaction."

She shook her head and said no more. She clipped a platinum leash onto the collar and gave me the handle.

"If anyone stops you and asks where you got the dog, don't say anything. If they want to know how you did it, just smile. If they want to buy if from you, walk on."

All clear.

"And no gossiping," she added when I was at the door.

Silent and serene, I walked through corridors, up and down stairways, along gravel paths, and over wooden bridges, reflected in the pretty ponds of the university gardens. Glances increased as I progressed. Shock, amazement, disgust, hilarity, appreciation, a whole range of emotions that I found ever more burdensome to bear.

Near the great central fountain, the rector, Kelb, greeted me with deference. He was with his Recognizer of Important People, a young lad with Tash's Syndrome who had been trained to recognize faces even when modified with heavy makeup, latex inserts, or even, as in my case, with hormonal changes. I acknowledged him with a nod and carried on walking. What an old meddler! He was staring unabashed at the dog.

After a few steps I felt a light touch on the shoulder. It was the Recognizer.

"Oh, Supreme Fruit of the Tree of Good and Evil, the Esteemed and Distinguished Archimandrite of All Students would like to know the race of the dog that you deign to show the world."

"And what did you reply?"

Vi was hoeing the furrows of the garden like she was weaving silken threads. I was observing her as I sat on the stone that covered the well, fiddling with a lock of my hair, which now fell onto my shoulders. I was very satisfied with my new look, but she wasn't paying any attention to me.

"I said: 'Elizabethan.'"

Not a muscle of her face even twitched. She gave no sign of being amused by my wittiness. Her melancholy, so deep rooted, so abysmal, attracted me like the edge of a cliff. Oh, to see a smile! To see the little pearls of her teeth peep through her velvet lips! The soft cushion of her smile would have been enough to make me dive headlong into the depths of pessimism.

"Don't you think it's time for you to explain what you want to do?" I said.

"I told you, I want to make money."

But it wasn't true, otherwise she would have checked to see that Pavlova's money was in her bank account instead of flowing through my veins in the form of hormones, but at that moment I was content to accept the lie.

"And you? What are you hiding?" she asked me as she continued with her weeding. "Why would the rector address you in such bombastic terms?"

I shrugged my shoulders.

"He's a pompous old goat with a theatrical vein. He must have confused me with someone else."

"That's just what you want to be, no? Someone else!"

"Yes, Ma'am, and I'm not ashamed to say so. I believe in change."

Vi raised her head and burst out laughing, but with no joy.

"You say 'change,' yet you think that it's always positive."

"Sure it is," I replied heatedly. "It's movement. Movement is better than staying still."

"It depends on the direction," she said.

That was the first time that Vi managed to dint my confidence.

"I improve. Each transformation makes me different from what I was before. It makes me original, unique."

I could hear myself speaking, and it was like listening to a stubborn boy wailing over his broken toy.

She didn't reply. She finished weeding in silence, and with her knife, she cut two heads of lettuce for dinner and dug up a few sweet potatoes.

As stipulated in the ad on the notice board, my remuneration consisted of light yet healthy meals, and we always ate them together.

From the description of her garden, you might think that the way Vi ate was simple, as terse and frugal as her conversation. You would be wrong. She was a complicated eater, very complicated. First of all, she didn't trust State vegetables, and she was right about that. She was lucky enough to own a patch of clean land, which she cultivated herself and which she watered using the water from her well. She lived mostly off raw vegetables picked on days of the waning moon, cut with a ceramic blade, and served on silver plates. She chewed each mouthful forty times. She had forbidden me to speak to her while she was eating. Even when she had finished eating I was only allowed to talk about happy and pleasant topics, lest I affect her digestion.

I devoured the fresh vegetables like a cabbage worm. I couldn't understand if it was a side effect of the hormones or if I really did especially like what she cultivated.

"Tomorrow you'll meet the person to whom you will deliver the *Elizabethan* dog," said Vi, dabbing at the corners of her mouth with her synthetic linen napkin. "You'll deliver this, too."

She handed me a magnetic card. It was a pass to get into the second year inorganic chemistry lectures.

Early next morning, I took the tram into the center of town.

Seated next to a window, I contemplated a row of detached homes, walls of pickled wood adorned with fretwork where they met the roofs, surrounded by majestic pine trees. I inhaled with pleasure the scent of balsam while the dog, cuddled up at my feet, attracted curious glances from the other passengers. I furtively examined their faces, all made from the same cosmeceutical mold—cheeks of the same curvature, eyebrows of the same thickness, embodied in every shade from plaster white to ash black but all rigorously smooth like sheets of packaging plastic. All of them, males and females, had high and spacious foreheads, a sign of intelligence obtained via the diathermocoagulation of the attachment of their hair.

Some, instead of looking at the dog, looked at me as I stood out amidst their standardized features: I was too tall, too well sculpted, I had too much hair, my lineaments too well marked.

At the address that Vi had given me, there was a pastry shop.

A blue and white awning shaded an elegant door of dark glass. I could smell wafts of caramelized sugar and roasted almonds. I was puzzled but trusted her blindly, or foolishly, I should say. I went in. The floor was made of natural fibers, the walls were rice paper, and there were pretty wooden racks to leave your shoes. Nope, they didn't bake cakes here.

I walked through the front room and found two men and a woman sitting on their heels, backs straight, hands in their laps, eyes half closed.

They were wearing splendid linen tunics cut in accordance with the rules of "humanist" tailoring so that the sleeves and the hems didn't impede the movement of the owner's arms and legs and conferred an air of elegance. They smelled of wet grass and dew, and their hair was adorned with tendrils of ivy and vines that grew in the pockets of the tunics.

"... three in Santé Square and another two in Fauxpas Boulevard," said one in an alarmed tone of voice.

"The distributors are everywhere now," said another one.

"And the kids are attracted irresistibly," added the woman.

"I think we should stick to the facts," continued the first one. "Our public condemnation has awakened many consciousnesses, but it's not enough."

"Rats! Rats!" replied the woman, raising her fist.

"I have the seeds," said the third one, holding onto a little cloth bag hanging round his neck.

"War against the State vegetable distributors!"

Ecologists!

If you think that you want to save the planet, then follow their advice.

I greeted them and sat down on the floor, making as

much noise as possible. First they just glanced at me, but after they noticed the dog, I had their full attention.

"A large, small marvel," commented the man with the seeds.

"Practical. No problem with encumbrance," added the woman. "Even if you have a small house, you can have a mastiff."

Swishing on its rails, a sliding door opened, and a little brunette woman in a flowery kimono appeared. She had a clean face without any outstanding features—like hundreds of others.

"Who's first?" she asked in an offhand manner.

The ecologist with the seeds stood up.

"I have a funeral to go to in three hours."

"Are there still people who have the bad taste to die?" asked the woman.

"He was a childhood friend," he replied defensively. "I'd like an expression that is fitting to the occasion."

With a gesture she beckoned him to follow. I scratched the dog's belly and impassively fielded the questions from the other two ecologists.

Half an hour later, the client reappeared—changed. The serene expression of a philosopher who has attained Nirvana had given way to a series of frown wrinkles. The muscles of his face were like wax melted in the heat ready to drip away from the frame of the bones to reveal the skull, the penultimate stage before leaping into the Void. On the lower eyelid there was a trembling line of tears, and the forehead was a corrugated field of parallel furrows. The man strode out boldly. I hoped that he would remember to control the rest of his body in an appropriate manner and not turn up at the funeral tap dancing.

The young lady motioned the other two to wait and beckoned to me.

On the other side of the sliding door, there was a chemical laboratory. There were two long ceramic counters covered with beakers, test tubes, and Bunsen burners. The air, saturated with sweet smells, ammonia, and flowery aromas, hit me like a punch in the face. In a corner was an antique barber's chair. A large oval mirror hanging over the chair reflected it completely.

"How did you manage to change his features?" I asked, in reference to the man who had just left.

She picked up a jar that contained a rust-colored gel, stuck a pipette into it, and sprayed a drop onto the corner of my mouth. I felt the muscle pulling down as if an invisible hand were pulling the skin downwards and holding it there with a pin.

"Bacteria," she replied, positioning me in front of the mirror. Half my mouth was drooping melancholically, and the other half was happy like a schizophrenic clown.

"It stings."

"He who wants to look sincere has to suffer a bit. In any case the effect wears off in about five hours. Once the bacteria have consumed the phosphorus in the culture, they can't survive for long."

I noticed that, on the cuff of her kimono, she wore a curious paper brooch in the shape of a frog.

Vi had told me, "She'll be the same as the others, but she won't renounce an original detail."

I gave her the dog and the pass for the chemistry lectures, which seemed kind of superfluous to me, given the resources she had here.

She took the lead and the magnetic card.

"I can make your eyebrows grow back in half an hour," she said.

"Why?"

"You lack a frame. The eyebrows are the frame of the emotions. Take them away and you are incomplete."

"I am already beautiful, thanks."

"Uh oh, it's more serious than I thought," she said.

"You may think it strange, but I paid money not to have eyebrows."

"Who's your cosmetic consultant? Fire him. He does a terrible job."

Before I could reply, the shameless hussy had pushed me out of the room.

"Next!" she called.

Microcephalous dwarf! Photocopy with legs! Eyeless aphasic!

I bathe in the envy of others, both male and female. They undress me with their eyes. They sniff the air I stir. I am *homo novus*, imperfect and luminous. I don't need to abide by the golden mean! My supreme virtue is expressed in a short yet powerful phrase: I am me. How many of you lot, copies of copies, can say the same?

I strode out quickly, my head heavy as if it had been beaten with hammers. The people out walking got out of my way and eyed me warily. All, all of them would have loved to capture me! I am a free being, and I swim against the current. The pain in my temples became unbearable.

I stopped in front of a public food distributor, the bugbear of the ecologists. Hot and cold soups, tasty looking pies, garishly colorful mixed salads. Ever since Vi had been providing for me, I hadn't touched the stuff. The State vegetables were devoid of vitamins and minerals. If you ate too many of them, they made your skin wrinkle and your intestines shrink.

Some people had even gone back to meat in order to avoid them.

They even said that they were addictive. Maybe it was true, but at that moment I didn't care. I rummaged in my pockets and found the pre-loaded card I kept for emergencies. I shouldn't have used it. I knew I was about to do something stupid, but I had to do it.

Card, slot, pay, mechanical clicking inside, three carrots in the delivery tray. Three beautiful, bright orange carrots with the tuft of greenery included. My new teeth, long and strong, crunched them with pleasure, and the tension left me. Even my headache went away.

Finals had started.

The poor students wandered aimlessly along the corridors holding their heads in their hands, moaning softly or gibbering; or they sat in corners chewing on coke bars, engrossed in reading up on how cyanobacteria split solar radiation, or some such. Shame that they forgot to turn the pages. Some tried to organize study groups—to no avail—and some bedded down in sleeping bags in the library with tins of liquid food and Benzedrine tablets.

Vi seemed calm. She had cancelled all new deliveries of the dogs and passed the time revising the fundamentals of obstetrics and gynecology, the final exam which she had to sit.

I, on the other hand, scrutinized my face in every reflecting surface that I could find. I would twist my mouth, puff out my cheeks, squeeze my eyelids. Was it just my imagination, or were my temples coming forward, naked and shameless? The curvature of my forehead was expanding, my sublime curls were receding, my smooth scalp was advancing, triumphant.

I could recognize the forehead of my father.

The almond shape of my eyes was becoming rounder, my sparse eyelashes were becoming thicker, my sinister look was giving way to a visus intelligens.

The eyes of my mother.

The hormonal magic was wearing off. I would have to go back to Aye and buy another hit of pituitary hormones, but my purse was empty. The Elizabethan dog had not provided any cash. I didn't understand why Vi had given it for free to the aesthetician, and I couldn't ask her—she had forbidden me to speak to her. Every morning she practiced dissecting virtual pelvises generated by an old surgery program. Every now and then the system crashed, and when she was rummaging around in the bladder looking for the uterus, the images would scatter in a fluttering confusion of colors and tissues and nerves and then it would reboot from the beginning and show an intact abdomen again. She never lost her patience and would start again, making her first incision with her laser scalpel. The program was so realistic that it was necessary to use the spreaders and clamps to hold back the flaps of the openings.

After a whole day spent studying, she would hook up to the Sphere and listen to her favorite preacher, Mister Lucky.

"Today I will speak to you of our enemies, dear brothers and sisters in prosperity."

Once again the lab was invaded by hundreds of virtual people sitting on the floor, their rapturous faces turned toward their idol.

"Our enemies are the unlucky people," he spat out angrily, "that feckless tribe of losers who just stand and wait to be afflicted by adversity, who patiently bear their illnesses, dismissals, assaults, and accidents. The modern Jobs who accept any blow of fortune, bow their heads saying, 'It's my fate,' saying, 'It's bad luck,' saying, 'C'est la vie!' No, brothers and sisters! It's not fate! It's their own fault! They are the only ones to blame for what happens to them!"

The speech was becoming interesting. I sat down to listen.

"The unlucky ones!" Each time he said those word it was like he was chewing on rotten food. "They are easily recognized, the hapless ones. They are the ones who, when newly born, end up in an incubator because they are weak, sickly, and premature. As children, they fall down a lot, break their bones, and seriously injure themselves. As teenagers, their peers look at them askance. During exams they get all the difficult questions—even ones about the footnotes! During job interviews they get the hostile selection panels. If they get married, it's to the wrong person, who will cause them suffering and unhappiness. Every abomination happens to the unfortunate ones."

"Poor people," I murmured ironically. Vi signaled me to keep quiet.

"And what's the paradox when we talk about these despicable people, my fortunate friends?"

Pause.

"They don't believe in Fortune!" shouted the apostle of good luck.

The audience gasped.

"Precisely. They maintain that human beings can create their destiny by themselves without the help of Our Great Goddess!"

"You underestimate hormones," I said loudly.

The preacher stared at me.

"There are some unbelievers amongst us. Do you have something to dispute with Fortune, lucky brother? You are healthy and good-looking and judging by your clothes, well off, too. Everything about you speaks of a favorite of the supreme goddess. What are your grievances?"

"Physiology determines luck," I replied, holding his fiery eyes. "The hypothalamus and the pituitary release and control the most important hormones that determine our behavior. The unlucky ones are weak because their posterior pituitary secretes little oxytocin, and this makes them incapable of facing up to the difficulties of life. They are looked on with little sympathy because they have little thyrotropin. Little thyrotropin means fatigue, muscular lassitude, no physical or mental vigor. You look at them and say, 'Insects!' For this reason their bosses think they are incompetent and give them boring and repetitive jobs."

"You believe in the body," replied the preacher, pointing at me with his index finger, arm outstretched.

"Is there anything else?"

He froze in a tragic pose, his mouth open and his hands

cupped over his ears in an attempt not to hear. Even the faces of the virtual public froze over in a display of shock and indignation. Vi had stopped the hookup.

"Who are you?" she blurted out. "The ghost of some twentieth-century doctor? You know nothing of behavioral physiology. You're just a welder. You emit sounds and think that they are thoughts. Go and clean the garden, go on!"

She waved her hands to shoo me out.

Humiliated by her words, instead of standing up, I scuttled away on all fours toward the sliding glass door that separated the lab from the outside. In the meantime Vi had muttered "sawbones" to herself indignantly and reestablished the link to the Sphere.

I weeded for an hour, and then she came out to join me. Her turquoise irises shone like pools of clear water at the bottom of the dark pits of the bags under her eyes. The meetings of Lucky Nation invigorated her like a flash of Resurrection. She approached and lifted up my hair as if she were looking for something near my face. A surge of heat pierced my breast. She took my right hand. Only then did I notice that the skin of her hands, small and slender, was marked by countless scars. I hadn't noticed before because Vi almost always wore latex gloves. Mastering the scalpel had cost her flesh and blood.

First she examined the back of my hands, then the palms. It seemed like she was looking for something.

"Acromegaly," she said

"That's your impression. I'm just well developed."

She flicked the tip of my nose with her finger.

"When you first arrived, you didn't have that bell pepper in the place of your nose. You had a nice normal nose in proportion to your face."

I blushed, more for having been touched by her rather than for what she had said.

"And your ears? You're always looking at yourself in the mirror. Have you looked at your ears recently? They've turned into enormous tropical shells. If the wind blew into them, you could use them as foghorns!"

I smiled, embarrassed.

"I just want to be me. I don't want to look like anyone else."

Vi sat down on the little wall around the well.

"What is *myself*?" she retorted. "Whoever heard of such a thing? How can you choose to be someone that you don't know?"

I rolled my hand and opened the Sphere—a great error— as unfortunately my photo files were there in my family page. I deleted headers and captions and showed her what I meant by "the real me."

"This is me at eight months."

My grandmother was holding me in her arms and was showing us our reflections in an old mirror in the living room of the house on the shores of the Mare Serenitatis. The photo had the grace of a candid snapshot and the solemnity of an official portrait: an old lady from high lunar society and a naked infant staring wide-eyed in the presence of an undeniable human phenomenon—recognition of oneself in a mirror.

"Here you can glimpse my real face," I continued. "Here I am really me."

"I don't understand what you mean. We are all a bit like Frankenstein: the nose of the father, the mouth of the mother, the eyebrows of the grandfather, the eyes of the grandmother. We are dolls made with bits of others sewn together and infused with life by the spark of conception."

"But in this photo I can still see the blank sheet before the genetics of my forefathers wrote over it!"

Vi crossed her arms and shook her shaven head.

"You're wrong. You're wrong about everything. It's in the psychic substrate that atrocities are committed."

She was always able to surprise me.

"You've never realized. No one ever does. It seems normal because it's invisible. You're trying to cancel your physical inheritance, but you're forgetting that parents implant their ambitions, their fears, their dreams, and their moral judgements. Whose are the thoughts we think?"

I was speechless.

"Here's an example," she went on. "Is my passion for creative surgery really *mine* or is it a sentiment of my father's?"

I leaned over the flower bed and heatedly ripped up some weeds then threw them onto the stones of the path. The prospect was making my head spin. Maybe even the search for myself could be an act foreign to the real me.

Vi made as if to leave.

"And luck?" I stopped her. "What's luck got to do with anything?"

"When you have something important to do, you have to curry favor with the gods."

A few days later Vi stuffed some fresh fruit and roasted vegetables into a natural fiber backpack.

"I have to ask you a favor," she said to me.

She knew that I would do anything for her.

"Defend the lab."

I sprang to attention and clicked my heels.

"They will get more than they bargained for, my commander!"

And off she went to face one of her most difficult finals, whistling Brahms's lullaby.

I bolted the door shut, fastened all the latches, and set the alarm.

Silence reigned all around me. All the other students had abandoned their strongholds to sit their finals. I spent the time lying down in the garden, cooling my back against the humid earth. If I got hungry I would reach out my hand, pull up a radish, and eat it raw, skin and top and all. I yawned with boredom and tried to hit the cabbage butterflies with my key ring laser. I liked the metallic noise they made when they fell onto the rocky path.

Asprillian insects is what they were called, in honor of the scientist who had invented them and released them into the environment. They were supposed to carry out pollination in place of the extinct insects, but they had turned out to be a rip-off.

On the third day the incessant chirping of a cricket drew me out of my lethargy, and the burglar alarm was saying that someone was trying to break into the lab through the door.

Barefoot, I approached the dark glass rectangle. On the other side I could hear a furtive scraping then suddenly two objects slid through the crack under the door. I squatted down and watched, fascinated. They were two skeletal fingers, flattened and formed by proximal and distal phalanges joined by a cartilaginous glue. The fingers were followed by fragments of carpal articulations without the metacarpals and a short ulna.

When the skeletal arm started to curl upwards toward one of the latches, I realized what this was all about. It was an osteoarticular jimmy.

I looked around. On a shelf was the perfect weapon with which to counterattack. The fingers had already slid back the first latch and were crawling toward the second when I sprayed them with extra-strength acetic acid. Sizzling, the bones crumbled away in seconds. The stink of burnt calcium must have reached the other side of the door, too, because the burglars quickly withdrew what was left of the arm and I heard them swearing under their breath.

"Go and do some studying, you useless good-for-nothings," I shouted.

There was a brief whispered confabulation on the other side of the door. The presence of a person inside made any more attempted burglary useless. The lab belonged to whomever was inside it. They left.

At sunset of the fifth day, Vi returned.

She threw down her empty backpack, flushed and euphoric, the medal of the final exam showing proudly branded onto a shoulder next to the ones for harmonic physiology and sympathetic biochemistry. She hugged me impulsively.

I wasn't expecting it, just like I wasn't expecting her to kiss me. On my cheeks, on my chin, on my mouth, a shower of kisses that became ever more insistent while her fingers fumbled under my shirt, undid zips, tore at clothing.

I know what you are thinking. Sly woman uses her cunt to ensnare a young man of good prospects. Nope, you're on the wrong track. Vi was not like that. There was never any premeditation in her acts, not in those acts. Her cup was full, the foam was overflowing, and I was glad that it was me that was getting wet on the floor between the surgical instrument trolley and the shelves of entrails. Her eyes were two glaucous slits in the twin moons of the bags under her eyes, her smell more feral than usual, five days that she hadn't washed. I groped her bony hips with my fingers, her buttocks hard as unripe apples, and among the hairs of her chalice, I broke through the skin of her fruit.

I'm lucky, I thought. I'm Fortune's favorite. I didn't call her. In fact, I ignored her. Nevertheless, she gave me what I wanted.

Lady Luck came—no lewd comments please—and then she left.

The next day Vi behaved as if nothing had happened. She was still floating on a cloud of exultation, but it wasn't directed at me. I had become invisible. At midmorning a delivery arrived from the university: twelve *sapiens sapiens* at various stages of development from pinkish tadpoles to big-headed larvae, all sealed up in glass jars. Vi lined them up on the counter and contemplated them as if entranced.

"Madame Pavlova will supply us with more puppies," she told me. "Let's get back to work."

We became a human cut-n-sew machine. She dissected fine slices of human craniums, eyes, and noses, and I welded them onto the faces of different animals. The mandatory step went from fetus to dog because the limbs of the slimy *sapiens sapiens* weren't developed enough to allow them to trot behind their owners. Twelve dogs and twelve fetuses. A tour de force that obliged us to combine and recombine the beasts in the most unusual ways. At twenty-five weeks the fetuses had a curious off-white down, especially around the eyebrows and upper lip, that made them resemble miniature doubles of Santa Claus. Vi made the most of this characteristic to mix them in to fox terriers that had come out badly (they didn't have any brown and black spots) to obtain animals with curly, ivory white hair with the characteristic long snout but with big languid, infantile eyes. You expected them to say "Hi" to you at any moment, but instead they whined and whimpered as the effects of the anesthetic wore off.

The wrinkled skin of the fetuses found its natural expression in the bulldogs, whose heads were softened with a less slobbery mouth and a smaller nose.

At the end of the last operation, my fingertips were aflame, smeared with blood, lymph, and some colloidal material where we conserved the little *sapiens*. I stuck them for five minutes into the dead material disintegrator and then into the sterilizer. The jets of peroxide burned my skin, and the muck under my fingernails flew away.

Vi staggered exhausted toward a little cupboard that was locked. She opened it, and two great loaves of bread fell onto her. She bit into one greedily. The whole cupboard was full of bread—bread with raisins, with nuts, with chocolate chips, made with white flour, with cornmeal, and with buckwheat; just the smell was enough to start you salivating.

Bread! Bread! After months of eating raw chicory and tomatoes! I devoured an entire baguette and then I dug into a fig loaf.

"You have to take them to the beauty clinic," Vi mumbled with her mouth full. "The dogs. You have to take them to the ecologists. As soon as they become adults."

I nodded my head without understanding. Became adults? The dogs or the ecologists?

Vi continued to stuff herself until her stomach, used to simple foods, couldn't take any more. She fell asleep, and, by the time I was putting the dogs into a regenerating fluid, she was already snoring.

A few days later, the aesthetician greeted me with a malevolent smile.

"So, you followed my advice! You look much better now."

In the lobby of the "pastry shop," there was a mirror. I looked at myself and screamed. I had gone back to looking like I did before! I threw the baskets into the girl's arms.

"Give me the money," I spat out.

She laughed.

"When I sell the goods."

"No, now! Immediately! Call your ecologist friends and tell them that the dogs are here."

I must have been very threatening or maybe desperate because she coughed up the cash.

A few hours later I was at the Institute of Biology looking for Aye with my pockets stuffed full of enough money to buy all the pituitary hormone on Earth!

"Aye?" said a student, batting her lashless eyelids. "Don't you know? He's gone."

"Gone? Gone where?"

She stretched out her arm and opened her fingers as if freeing an insect trapped in her fist.

"Into the world, into life. He has graduated."

I never thought that that lazy good-for-nothing actually studied seriously.

"Listen, I need pure hypophysial extract. Can you get me some?"

She looked at me, stunned, and then burst out laughing, showing me her toothless gums.

I tried to get to the exit, but in the meantime I had been surrounded by a crowd of students who were trying to suck my toes, grasping my legs but slipping off of the impermeable plastic with which I had protected myself. I kicked out at those vile beings and tried my question on some other biology students—there were still some who walked upright and with dignity.

"Do you think that if I had any pituitary hormone to analyze, I would give it to you?" retorted one.

Exasperated and tired, I shuffled out into the garden.

I avoided the fountains and mirrors of water. The last thing I wanted to see was my *familiar* image. I would have attempted to drown myself.

At sunset the sound of drumming drew me toward the center of the park. A student party had started. A hermaphrodite from pharmacology sold me a box of serotonin sweets, which I devoured avidly, and I immediately fell into a euphoria that stayed with me for the duration of the party.

I returned to the laboratory in the wee small hours. Vi had risen and was sitting in the garden, still half stunned from her bread binge, with her elbow poised over a cauliflower and caressing the crisp, young lettuces with her hand. She raised her eyes, darker than usual, and smiled at me, only just slightly curving her pallid lips. That smile was not for me. It was the reflex of an intimate secret joy, but I didn't understand then. I couldn't understand.

"It's you," she said.

"No, it's not me. I'm the other one, my parent's creation."

"You only have to decide to use your freedom."

"You change reality with your scalpel, I do it with my method."

"There is no real you to which you can return," replied Vi. "When will you realize that?"

"I am a welder," I replied. But it was a half-truth. I could join, and I could separate. I struggled to keep together the fragments of the "real me" without deciding to separate myself from my family, from the dregs of thought, from all the mistaken ideas built up over the years of false behaviors.

She ruffled the leaves of the lettuce, and then she burped, but quietly.

"There are choices to be made. Each choice, a renunciation; each renunciation, a modification."

At certain moments Vi seemed to be full of wisdom and foresight. To look at her, I would have said we were of the same age, but who can tell how old anyone is these days? We are all young and foolish.

The full moon looked down at us over the top of the wall. The lights of Lunaria, the capital, nullified the shadows of the Seas and twinkled like a handful of sequins stuck to the face of a ruddy cheeked student ready to go out on the town.

I curled up with my head on my knees, oppressed by so much light. I was in a dark mood, and I only wanted darkness around me.

In two months dog mania broke out.

The ecologists had each been going about at the end of a leash, and at the other end of each leash was one of our dogs: a wizened stovepipe that hobbled along on short inverted legs, paws turned inward, and a round, puffed up face with a mouth like a duck's ass under large, curious, and attentive eyes, as only an animal hungry for knowledge of the world can have.

Vi's creativity exploded. She made neo-dogs with velvety nails so they couldn't scratch their owners' furniture and clothes; neo-dogs with fringed ears for those nostalgic for Westerns; microcephalus lapdogs with three heads that could suck a rudimentary thumb; and even a Chihuahua with a mouth in the shape of a vulva and a tiny penis for a tail. The vulva went yap-yap, and the little dick wagged when the dog saw its owner.

The production of dogs continued at a constant rate, and every time we made a new "model," Vi sent it to the aesthetician. I never did find out her name nor were we ever introduced. I called her Phryne, sure that she would be too ignorant to catch the mockery.

Phryne sold the neo-puppies, kept her commission, and gave me the rest of the money, which I didn't know what to do with. Without Aye, without any pituitary hormones, I avoided all reflecting surfaces and all social events. When I wasn't working, I wandered around the department reading the graffiti on the walls before the self-cleaning paint could eliminate them.

A musical surgery band looking for patients with stones in the gallbladder promised that one jam session would dissolve them. I thought it more likely they'd bore my balls off. A string quartet offered its services for realigning vertebrae and for improving the state of the inter-disk cartilage. They claimed to be able to modify my facial features by bowing in a quick four-four time, and I would have my old face restored without any of the false features of my forebears. I took down their room number, but then I had second thoughts. The music would only be a temporary fix, not a treatment.

As I was returning to the laboratory, I spied a familiar face in the middle of a crowd of students who were pushing and shoving, trying to get into the Chemistry lecture room.

"Phryne, what are you doing here?"

She turned away, pretending not to know me.

"A person like you should be giving a chemistry lecture, not going to listen to one."

Eighty eyes were suddenly staring at her. One second she was a student like all the others, the next she was like a supernatural phenomenon. She felt the eyes on her, oppressing her. With her head bowed she squeezed my arm and dragged me to a corner.

"Are you crazy? If they find me out, I risk being crippled!"

I had seen them around. People had been crippled, hacked, and mutilated, depending on the department that they had tried to infiltrate without being matriculated at the university.

"I want to produce cosmetics," she went on, "and I don't have the basics. The chemists are very jealous of their knowledge."

"I need your help."

"I can make you ugly. It's the new fashion. Ugly is the new sexy."

I wasn't even listening to her.

"If I wanted a higher forehead, for example, or a more pronounced jaw, what would you advise me?"

Phryne weighed me up, sucking in her cheeks.

"I would need double-action bacteria, myolytic and myo-reconstructive."

"How long would their effect last?"

"Bring me some more dogs and we can talk about it," she replied.

Phryne analyzed my cranium and my muscles with an instrument similar to an ultrasound machine. She obtained a 3-D image on which she worked with her fingers, following my instructions. She lengthened my eyes, puffed out my cheeks, made my mouth more subtle, the cheekbones lower, the chin rounder—she added a dimple in the center on her own initiative—until all those features transformed me into a different person.

"Perfect," I exclaimed when she had finished.

She grimaced.

"An aged baby," she muttered.

I lay back in the barber's chair and underwent the treatment: massage with smelly ointment, hundreds of micro-injections. It was like being attacked in the face by a swarm of bees covered with a mysterious substance, which, when it dried, pulled at every muscle fiber, forcing me to open my mouth wide. Phryne, unconcerned, stuck a saliva ejector into it and continued working.

She put the 3-D image over my head and with a sort of plastic spatula, began to push, pull, press, and curl, making my real features match up with the virtual model. My face felt as soft as the icing on a cake. And I wasn't totally wrong in likening myself to a dessert. After having shaped me to her complete satisfaction, she placed my chair parallel to the floor and stuck my head into a horizontal cylinder fitted with a porthole —basically an oven for human soufflés. Slow cooking for at least one hour.

When she pulled me out, I asked her for a mirror.

"Don't speak," she warned me. "You're still hot."

In fact, my skin burned as if I had scalded myself with boiling water. I could feel my cranium pulsating with each breath like a meringue about to crack.

She handed me a round mirror, and I greeted the new me. On the other side of the glass, my reflection reciprocated by widening his eyes, stolid and happy like the rector's Recognizer with Tash's syndrome.

"You have to rest for at least 24 hours," said Phryne. She made me get up, took me to another room, and after helping me lie down on a litter, she left.

I sighed. On a little table were some magazines. I picked one up, *L'ami du chien*. The cover article was singing the praises of "The Age of the Dog."

"A man and his dog," we say, because nowadays the dog is all that one can have in terms of love. Human beings are no longer willing to sacrifice time and passion

for other human beings. Why love another when I can love myself?

There were also a few pictures, some of badly made chimeras twisted, patched up, the tongue too long, the teeth too big for the mouth, the ears misaligned, the animal-like snouts too menacing or stultified by the purity of the alleles.

I turned over the page and almost fell out of the litter in surprise.

The centerfold was of one of our dogs. An ecologist was holding the dog in his arms. A proud neo-father with his neo-dog.

The round cranium and wide forehead of the dog dominated the picture. Two subtle arches of white fluff framed the translucent eyelids from fetus to the twenty-fourth week; the delicate snub nose stuck out all rosy like a bud, and the mouth was drooling, showing the baby carnivorous teeth. Oh, those teeth! They cost me blood, sweat, and tears every work session. Vi would extract them from miniature puppy bull terriers, cutting into the jaw, and I would prepare a channel in the bone of the fetus and insert those tiny four-cusp pebbles, slimy with blood and mucus. Then I would weld them into place. They would always slip out of my fingers and roll over the floor of the lab and get stuck in the cracks between the broken tiles.

The dog was smiling angelically, leaning on its forepaws, which were covered with white hair. Seraphim model. All it was missing was a pair of wings on its back.

The article was gushing about the new species of *canis canis*, whose features made it the ideal companion for whomever wanted a guardian angel in the house. The following pages contained images of other models: the Napoleon, with a massive head and an expression of insolent boredom in the wrinkles of its mouth; the Owl, with haunting eyes in which a glimmer of human intelligence could be discerned; and the most popular, the Attila, for which Vi had used some Tasmanian devil puppies—long bite, fangs, opaque pupils, and slit eyes.

I stayed at Phryne's for three days, sleeping and resting. At the end of the third day, she gave me an ointment and kicked me out.

I set off for the department, and during my walk, I was able to experience the force and extent of the canine phenomenon firsthand or, better yet, "firstfoot."

The hour before sunset was when people took their dogs out for a walk.

The preferred meeting place was the Boulevard de la Merde, a mile and a half of marble sidewalks and lawns bordered with cypresses.

Apart from our animals, the most popular articles on display were air stilts—two long, metal box-like affairs which fastened to the shoes using straps like roller skates without wheels. Clicking your heels together would raise you over a foot above the surface. The dog owner could thus walk carefree, greet other owners, look around, relaxed and smiling while lengthening the leash to allow nature to take its course.

But not me.

I was the only one unfortunate enough not to own any air stilts.

Sidewalks, roads, and lawns were covered in a layer of canine excreta, an extended geology of fresh shit over dry shit over even more compacted unbreakable shit. It stuck to my sandals and with each step, increased in thickness under the soles. I think I must have gained seven or eight inches in height.

However, since the facial makeover had altered my olfactory membranes, I could hardly smell the stench that emanated from the ground, making me think that maybe I ought to believe in luck.

I met Rector Kelb again, who was taking his Napoleon (Cerberus sub-variant) for a walk, three fetal crania on which we had implanted Doberman ears and greyhound necks, all mounted on a bulldog body. He didn't greet me. Phryne's bacterial mask had rendered me invisible.

I don't know how I managed to cross that disgusting mile and a half, but I eventually returned to the lab.

Vi was engaged in a heated argument with a man whom I had never seen before.

"I don't believe that."

After having listened in silence for nearly an hour, the Judge stopped Kieser's story, waving her hands impatiently and signaling the stenographer to underline that last phrase.

The interrogation room seemed to wake up as if from a spell. The Captain, a man with curly hair, moved away from the wall that he had been leaning against the whole time. The young Lieutenant, the top button of his uniform tight against his throat, made as if to stretch.

Kieser shrugged. "I didn't know who he was."

"But you knew everything about Victoire Mizanekristos." The Judge, a woman with white hair, enrobed in a purple toga, leaned toward Kieser, awaiting his answer. His skin was fresh and shining while still showing some expressive wrinkles around the eyes and mouth.

"I thought she was called Vikananda Theodora Stern," replied Kieser.

The Judge made an impatient gesture with her hand.

"Why did the man come to see you?"

The Judge gestured toward a glass of water on the tray on the table, and the stenographer, solicitous, handed it to her.

"Rumors were circulating. Someone must have told him where to go to get a fashionable dog."

"Did Vi not introduce you?" interjected the Lieutenant. "You went into the lab and ... nothing? She didn't say or do anything?"

The Judge almost choked on her water, the Captain winced. Kieser gave the Lieutenant a short cold glance and then looked away.

"I meant to say ..." stammered the Lieutenant. "Oh, Sidereal, Immense, Unattainable—"

The Captain made a peremptory gesture; and the Lieutenant shut up, and then he made him follow him out of the room.

"What a boor!" murmured Kieser

"We are most sorry, Oh Golden Fruit of the Tree of Good and Evil. I beg for your indulgence."

The door had remained ajar, and the angry voice of the Captain could be heard from the corridor.

"I chose you because you know the protocol! You can't speak to him as if he were a purse snatcher!"

With a gesture the Judge ordered the stenographer to close the door. The room was once again filled with pregnant silence as before the incident.

"So," began the Judge, "you went back to the lab, and you saw Victoire engaged in a conversation with a stranger. Can you describe him to us, Oh Sublime Jewel?"

"Tall, lanky, lively, white hair. Natural hair. When I entered, he glanced at me distractedly. I think he must have thought I was Vi's assistant—sometimes the University assigns one to the head of a lab."

The Captain and the Lieutenant came back into the room, trying to make as little noise as possible.

"Did you know who that man was?" continued the Judge.

"No."

The Judge squinted at him. "I'll tell you who he was. He was the cleverest thief of the *Civil Society* organization.

Kieser's face showed that he had registered the information but nothing more.

"You heard their conversation," continued the Judge.

"Only the last exchange. Vi said to him, 'So, are we agreed

for the day after tomorrow?' He replied, 'I recommend the Seraphim,' and then they shook hands."

The Captain and the Judge exchanged a glance.

"They had just reached an agreement," summarized the Judge. "A verbal agreement."

Kieser shrugged his shoulders. "If you say so."

The Judge straightened up, irritated.

"The perfect laboratory assistant. You didn't see anything, you didn't hear anything, and you didn't understand anything that was happening."

"Careful how you speak, Your Rightness. I have voluntarily offered my collaboration and could just as easily change my mind."

"You knew of that obscene exchange," she said, looking him in the eye.

"Are you accusing me of complicity, Your Rightness?"

The atmosphere in the room had become very tense. The Captain intervened.

"Would you like something to drink, Oh Golden Fruit of the Tree of Good and Evil?"

Kieser relaxed and leaned back in the chair.

"Yes, please. I'll have a *Thousand Meters* tea."

The Captain's face puckered up in consternation.

"Oh, how silly of me," said Kieser. "I forgot we're not on the Moon. A cold melota will do fine."

The Captain turned to the Lieutenant and sent him in search of the drink.

"Carry on with your story," said the Judge, turning to Kieser.

After the mysterious man had left, Vi looked me in the face.

"Does it hurt?" she asked.

"It's a bit tight in my cheeks, but I don't feel any pain."

It was true. The bacteria worked discretely, but I still wasn't happy with the new me. I felt slow and distracted. I made the same mistake twice on the easy dissection of the ears of an Italian Pomeranian, and Vi had to intervene with her scalpel. It was necessary to redo some welds and cover them with thicker hair than usual.

She didn't say anything, and she didn't seem impatient or annoyed. She remedied all my mistakes and in the end obtained what had been requested of her: a Seraphim with the ears and proud expression of a Napoleon, and the teeth of an Attila.

Three days later, the man who had commissioned the beast turned up to take possession of it. The dog still wasn't in a fit state to be transported, but he insisted. He was in a hurry —that, I remember well—in a big hurry. He was constantly looking over his shoulder as if he was expecting a pursuer to jump out at him at any moment.

He left a parcel. No money. Only a heavy object wrapped up in dark paper on which two warnings had been stamped: *Fragile* and *This End Up*.

Vi wasn't in. She had gone to the library to consult some texts on creative surgery. I was too involved in the study of my new head, deducing that inside my cranium there had to be a walnut-sized lump of grey matter. Maybe the "real me" had dried up due to excessive thinking. Maybe I had buzzed around the same flower too much. The result was a head like a wilted flower wearing an expression of dazed stupidity.

The fact is, I took what I was given, and I handed over what I was meant to without bothering too much about what I was taking and handing over.

As I said, I had no idea who that man was. You say that he was a thief from the Civil Society, and I don't doubt it for a minute; but even if I had known that at the time, how could I have deduced what Vi was up to?

When I gave her the parcel, it was like Vi was frozen. By now I knew her well enough to know that the thicker the crust of ice over her emotions, the more violent and wild were the emotions being covered up.

I was seated next to the well, fretting about my mistake when she threw a sponge impregnated with a dense liquid into my lap.

"Wipe off your face. I need you."

The sponge smelled of salt water, of sun-dried sand, of fresh algae. I rubbed it all over my face, and in a few moments, Phryne's work crumbled. I was afraid. It seemed that the flesh itself was peeling away from the bones, and I tried to stop it falling off with my hands. I found my fingers dirty with a transparent goo that stuck to my skin and that tried to grasp onto the derma. I rubbed my hands and face with the sponge and could almost hear the bacteria screaming. My idiocy died with them.

Vi was waiting for me at the operating table.

She had already anaesthetized some Dogue de Bordeaux puppies, French mastiffs with champagne-colored coats, too light to be considered for the standard of purity. The scalpels gleamed, all lined up on the sterile tray. I smelled an unusual scent in the air under the big lamp.

Without a word, Vi indicated the mask and headgear. I put them on and the creation began.

"Was it then that she opened the parcel?" asked the Judge.

"No."

"Was there not also a fetus together with the puppies on the operating table?"

"As always. We kept them in the cultivation basin."

"And did you not make a connection between what the stranger delivered and this new fetus?" insisted the Judge.

"No, why should I have done so? The shelves were overflowing with midgets in cultivation. Vi had gotten top marks in gynecology so she got lots of leftovers. I thought it was one of those."

"What did it look like?"

Kieser shrugged his shoulders.

"The same as the others. Wrinkled skin, squashed nose, thin fingers, big head ..."

"Did you realize that it was healthy?"

"Most of the ones that they gave us were whole without any visible deformities. How could I imagine that Victoire was using her ..."

Kieser stopped and swallowed a gulp of his melota.

"... own brother," concluded the Judge.

Vi dissected the dogs' snouts, obtaining a series of slices of muscle, dark and folded up. Then she exposed the jaw of the fetus and broke it into four parts with a small hammer. She made me weld each bone to the tendons of the canine resections, overlapping and alternating the layers—one human, one canine—in such a way that the snout was a perfect blend of both and facilitated by the human doliocephalous cranium.

Then she transplanted the eyes of the dog into the eye sockets of the fetus.

This surprised me. Usually we took out a human part and inserted it into a canine head. I think she wanted to maintain the original aspect of the fetus as much as possible. She made me remove the paws of a puppy, and after reinforcing them with titanium inserts, she ordered me to weld them to the torso of the fetus. She removed a few canine fingers and replaced them with human ones, such that the indexes were recognizable in the front paws.

She followed the same procedure for the skin. She removed portions of dog dermis and transferred the fur to the fetus while leaving some areas naked where the rosy skin of a newborn would grow instead of animal hair.

We worked for many hours. I couldn't say how many. She was sweating, and every now and then I had to wipe her forehead and temples. I realized then that the strange smell in the lab was coming from her. It was a smell of clean skin, clean hair, with a hint of shampoo. She had washed herself before the operation.

Lastly, I bandaged up the neo-dog as usual and impregnated the bundles with regenerative liquid to speed up the healing.

Three days later, it could stand up on its paws and bark.

"It barked?" repeated the Judge.

"Well, it made a noise similar to 'woof woof.'"

The Judge stood up, walked over to a keypad, and pushed a button. On the wall in front of Kieser, a rectangular panel rose up, revealing a window onto another room: a small padded cell. On the other side of the glass, there was a four-legged animal. From afar it looked like a poodle shaved in alternating areas where some patches were covered in curly hair and others were pink and bald and delicate. A shudder would convulse it periodically every time it opened its mouth.

The Judge pressed another button, and the room was filled with a high-pitched, staccato sound. It started like a wail—*waa, waa*—the classic sound of a newborn baby, but then the vowel sound transformed, became rounder and more drawn out—*uuuuu*—like the sad howling of a distant coyote.

The creature was turning round and round in circles, stopping only to make its sound. It moved on four legs, but the way in which it moved its forepaws resembled the uncoordinated attempts at crawling of a child. The human fingers that emerged from the hairy paws confirmed this impression. All at once it stopped chasing its tail, went to a corner, raised its leg, and pissed. The drops of urine turned into tiny golden butterflies that fluttered around the room while the animal chased them, barking loudly.

The sound made the butterflies turn into little biscuits, and the golden cloud fell to the floor. The hungry creature was upon them at once, emitting a curious yelp of satisfaction halfway between a high-pitched noise from the throat and an infantile gurgling.

The Judge pointed to the creature on the other side of the window.

"You delivered this neo-dog to Victoire's parents."

Kieser stretched out his arms.

"How could I know? Vi gave me an address and told me to take payment on delivery as usual. They were clients just like all the others. At the door a robot appeared— made of pots and pans with two vacuum cleaners for legs and two umbrellas for arms. People buy all sorts of domestic robots these days. I certainly didn't think it was a magic puppet. Besides, who remembered that her parents were Barum?"

The Judge leaned over the electronic tablet in front of her and scrolled down nervously, looking for something.

"The Mizanekristoses decided to have another child using artificial fertilization. A week ago their fetus disappeared from the incubator of the fertility clinic."

"I only know that there was a dog to deliver to a client. I gave the basket to the robot, and it gave me a velvet bag. I understood immediately what it contained so I didn't advertise my presence in public. At a certain point I couldn't resist, and I poured the contents of the bag into the palm of my hand."

He shook his head, still incredulous at the memory of what he had seen, and took another sip of his melota.

"Vi told me that she wanted to make money. Well, she succeeded. Ten pretty, little rocks. I'd say at least three carats each. Very pure, the color was a D, maximum transparency, classic brilliant cut, expertly executed."

"Where are the diamonds?" asked the Judge.

"I gave them to Vi. The next day she left the lab and disappeared."

"Victoire Mizanekristos has the ability of vanishing into thin air without using magic powers. Three years ago she abandoned her family without leaving any traces."

"Did her parents report her disappearance?" asked Kieser.

The Judge had a moment of uncertainty and then resumed talking.

"Her parents sustain that Victoire was a difficult child from the time she was very young. They have tried several times to cure her of—"

"Cure her? Vi is healthy and normal."

"Victoire is unable to move a chair without physically touching it, an action that any Barum child can carry out at the age of five, but she has always refused to undergo the spells that could have helped her."

"Ah, I see," said Kieser. "The Mizanekristos wanted a child with magic powers. Their wish has been granted. They will grow old in the company of a creature that will love them unconditionally. It will wag its tail happily every time it sees them, will never demand anything from them, and will stay with them forever."

Kieser stopped, a bit breathless, and finished off his melota from the glass.

The Judge and the Officers have convened in the room next door. They're arguing loudly, so loudly that I can't help hearing what they're saying.

"I would like to hold him," said the Judge, "but the forty-eight hours are up."

"Complicity?" says the Lieutenant. "Complicity in kidnapping a fetus and in mutilating an infant?"

Apart from not knowing etiquette, the Lieutenant doesn't even know the law. Amusing.

"The boy's family was on the Moonflower," replies the Captain. "Half the Moon belongs to them."

"He allowed himself to be found," insists the Lieutenant.

CLELIA FARRIS

"The card he used to buy the vegetables, his photo taken in the Sphere—it was all calculated."

"There's nothing I can do!" says the Judge. Angry. Exasperated. "He's protected by lunar immunity."

"He helped the woman to get revenge," insists the Lieutenant, "and we are part of that revenge. He wanted us to know *who* kidnapped the fetus!"

They don't have any hard evidence.

I dealt with Pavlova.

I took the dogs to Phryne.

I never spoke to anyone about what we did in the lab. No gossiping.

My testimony is the only validation of Vi's guilt, but Terrestrial law only admits Terrestrial witnesses.

In the other room, there's a long silence.

"What will we say to the Barum?" says the Captain.

Another silence.

"We'll say ... we'll tell them to keep the dog and to try to educate it like a child. Maybe, with the right teachers ..."

I bite my lip to keep from laughing out loud.

Well, I'm done here. I stand up, I stretch, and nod goodbye to the doorman, who opens the door and bows low as I leave. One who knows how to behave in my presence.

I cross the courtyard and exit.

I think that Vi's parents are idiots.

A silver Yang—Moon color—is parked on the other side of the street.

Vi is a genius. And they were lucky to have such a daughter. But it's not enough to be lucky. You also have to have the intelligence to recognize Luck, and they didn't have that. Serves them right. They deserve the neo-dog. Vi has shown them that birth isn't everything. She made them see that it's possible to be whoever you want—despite genetics.

She even showed me.

The driver gets out, takes off his cap, and opens the door.

166

"You go in the back, Robur. I feel like driving."

He obeys, and I take the steering wheel.

Vi jumps into the front next to me. The familiar smell of her sweat makes me feel at home.

"How did it go?"

"Good."

"Did they believe you?"

"No. But I'm lucky."

I adjust the rearview mirror and steal a quick glance at myself.

I look very much like me.

ACKNOWLEDGEMENTS

I want to thank my Italian editor, Francesco Verso, who encouraged me to write the short stories that are included in this anthology. I must also thank Marcella Cancedda for her merciless editing and for forcing me to rewrite these stories from top to bottom.

I'd like to express my gratitude to Rachel Cordasco and Jennifer Delare for their marvelous translations.

Finally, my sincerest thanks to Bill Campbell, who loves my stories enough to publish them in the United States.

ABOUT THE AUTHOR

Born in Cagliari in 1967, Clelia Farris graduated in psychology with a thesis on epistemology. A favorite with both readers and experts, she is considered one of Italy's best science fiction authors. She won the Fantascienza.com Award with *Rupes Recta*, the Odyssey Award with *No Man Is My Brother*, and the Kipple Prize with *The Weighing of the Soul*. In 2012 she published *The Justice of Isis*, set in the same futuristic Egypt of *The Weighing of the Soul*. In 2015 she published the novella, *Creative Surgery*, which has been included in the anthologies, *Storie dal domani 2* and Rosarium Publishing's *Future Fiction: New Dimensions in International Science Fiction and Fantasy*. She was a finalist for the Urania Mondadori Award 2016 with her story, "Uomini e Necro." Her stories have also been published Italian and in international magazines such as *Robot, Fantasy Magazine, Future Science Fiction*, and *Strange Horizons*.